"HOW COULD YOU!"

The words burst from Rex, deep and low as if they were spoken in the extremity of pain.

"Do understand," Fenella pleaded; "you've got to understand."

"And if I don't?"

He spoke the words harshly, then suddenly his hands went out towards her, taking her by the shoulders, drawing her nearer to him.

"I loved you," he said. "I loved you more than I believed it possible to love any woman —and now this has happened. It isn't your fault and it isn't mine; Fate has been too strong for us. . . ."

Pyramid Books

by

BARBARA CARTLAND

THIS TIME IT'S LOVE

Barbara Cartland

PYRAMID BOOKS ▲ NEW YORK

THIS TIME IT'S LOVE

A PYRAMID BOOK

Copyright © 1977 by Barbara Cartland

Pyramid edition published May 1977

Printed in the United States of America

Pyramid Books are published by Pyramid Publications (Harcourt Brace Jovanovich, Inc.). Its trademarks, consisting of the word "Pyramid" and the portrayal of a pyramid, are registered in the United States Patent office.

Pyramid Publications
(Harcourt Brace Jovanovich, Inc.)
757 Third Avenue, New York, N.Y. 10017

AUTHOR'S NOTE

I wrote this book originally in 1944. Nearly all the characters were taken from real people and incidents which had occurred during the war. I knew many of the artists who lived in Chelsea during the twenties and thirties, whose behavior shocked and intrigued us.

Today the colourful personalities like Simon Prentis would evoke little comment but at the time they were sensational.

"The dark quick stream of passion swirling
    past,
Widening ripplewise to form
Its own tumultuous tide;
Passion immersed, encompassed by itself,
Too deep, too dark for comprehensive thought,
Yet lo! a gleaming shaft of sun can find
An echoing light;
Gold tip the crested waves, pierce through
    the sombre depths.
To love!
The love which all must seek because
It is Divine."

CHAPTER ONE

1943

The old-fashioned door-bell pealed in the passage.

"One cupful of flour . . one ounce of butter . ." Fenella repeated to herself.

The bell pealed again . .

"Oh, bother!"

She walked to the kitchen door, wiped her hands on the towel hanging behind it and went to answer the bell. As she reached the hall Nannie appeared at the top of the stairs.

"Is that you, dearie?" she asked. "I was afraid no one had heard it."

"It's all right, Nannie," Fenella called. "Don't come downstairs."

"Good morning. Could I speak to the owner?"

The sunshine glittered in Fenella's eyes, blinding her a little, so that it took her a moment to see who was standing outside the door. The voice was low and rather charming with a cool note of authority in it.

Fenella blinked and saw a tall man in uniform; behind him, waiting in the drive, was a camouflaged car with a uniformed driver at the wheel.

"Won't you come in?" she asked, after a moment's hesitation.

"Thank you."

The officer walked past her and stood in the shade of

the hall waiting, she fancied, a little impatiently for her to lead the way. She smiled at him, then seeing his expression realized that he had mistaken her for the maid.

It was not surprising, Fenella thought swiftly; she had been cooking all the morning and she was wearing a big enveloping white apron, now slightly stained and crumpled, and her sleeves were rolled up above the elbow.

"This way," she said demurely.

She led him into the small sitting-room where the fire, lit only a short time ago, was still somewhat dark and unwelcoming.

"I will tell Miss Prentis you are here," Fenella said in what she hoped was a respectful retainer's voice.

With that she shut the door on him.

'I wonder what he wants?' she thought. 'Anyway, it will do him good to cool his heels a bit while I get ready.'

In her bedroom Fenella powdered her nose and smoothed the waves of her dark hair on either side of her forehead, pulled down the sleeves of her yellow jumper and slipped on the leaf-green cardigan which toned with her checked skirt.

'Now I look more like the occupier,' she told herself as she proceeded slowly and with some dignity downstairs to the sitting-room.

She opened the door and saw that her guest had his back to her. He was standing looking down at the fire, his hands holding on to the mantelpiece, his coat and cap put tidily on a chair near the window. He held the rank of Major she noted swiftly.

'Good shoulders,' Fenella thought to herself appraisingly, and as he turned—'Good looking,' then added: 'But it's a hard face, hard and unyielding.'

"How do you do," she said out loud. "I'm Fenella Prentis. I think you wanted to see me."

He stared at her for a moment before he smiled, a slow, attractive smile which transformed his face.

"I must apologize," he said coming forward and holding out his hand. "It was the apron that deceived me."

10

"It was quite understandable," Fenella said, "and if you took me for the servant you were quite right. It's my job nowadays."

"I hope you will forgive me," he said releasing her hand. "And now, if I may introduce myself, my name is Ransome and I have called to ask if I may billet some of my officers here."

Fenella stared at him in dismay.

"But that's impossible!" she said. "Who'd look after them?"

"I was going to ask you to do that," he answered, "although I hope it will only be for a short time.

"We are building a camp the other side of the village as you may have heard. We expected it to be ready when we moved in, but unfortunately our expectations have not been realized.

"I can accommodate most of the men in the farmers' barns, but there don't seem to be many houses in the village suitable for the officers."

"There are very few," Fenella agreed. "What about Wetherby Court?"

"Sir Nicholas Coleby's place?" Major Ransome asked. "I'm afraid that's too far away. You see, we have to be on the spot and at the moment we are extremely limited with petrol."

"But I don't know how we can have anyone here," Fenella said. "You see, the house is tiny and my Father comes home on leave fairly frequently so that I can't offer you his room."

"He's in the Services?" Major Ransome asked.

Fenella nodded.

"Yes, in the R.A.F., although not operational; he's in charge of the camouflage department at the Air Ministry."

"Prentis," Major Ransome repeated the name thoughtfully, "I suppose your Father isn't by any chance Simon Prentis?"

Fenella smiled.

"That's right."

"Good gracious! He's a very famous person. I didn't

11

know he lived in this part of the world, I thought he had a studio in London."

"Oh, he gave that up years and years ago," Fenella said. "He couldn't bear the noise of the traffic and the feeling of being cramped, so he bought this house. It was only a farm then and he added on the barn to make himself a studio.

"It looks big from the outside but that's due to the barn—the rest of the house is really very small. But I'll show it to you if you like."

"That's very kind of you," Major Ransome said. "You must understand, Miss Prentis, that I hate having to billet ourselves on reluctant civilians, but it has to be done. We have to sleep somewhere."

"But of course."

Fenella led the way from the sitting-room into the small, oak-beamed hall, then opened a door on the right.

The building which was Simon Prentis' studio had been beautifully converted from a three-century old barn using the oak beams wherever possible.

The windows which were let into both sides of it managed to admit the maximum amount of light without being unduly obtrusive.

The floor was polished and covered with soft-toned rugs; there was an open fireplace and plenty of big comfortable-looking armchairs and inviting sofas.

There was, as might be expected, a model's throne and an easel, but otherwise the room was very unlike the usual artist's studio.

"It's charming," Major Ransome exclaimed.

"My Father is rather different from most painters," Fenella said. "He likes to work with everyone round him."

"It's certainly a marvellous place," Major Ransome said approvingly, "and I shall hope very much to have the privilege of meeting your Father. I'm a great admirer of his works—in fact I'm proud to say that I own one of his pictures."

"Which one?" Fenella asked curiously.

" 'A Girl Laughing'. It was the picture of the year in 1936."

"Oh, I remember it," Fenella said. "Inez modelled for that—it was painted just before Daddy married her."

She spoke coolly and dispassionately, but Major Ransome gave her a quick glance before saying:

"She was certainly lovely; I've never seen hair of such a wonderful colour."

"Yes, Daddy always chooses red-heads as his models—but of course you know that."

"I've always heard that was so," Major Ransome replied; "but I didn't know if it was just gossip."

"Oh, no, it's quite true," Fenella answered. "Daddy only admires red-haired women. Moo and I are a great disappointment to him."

"Moo?" the Major questioned.

"My sister. She's at school now, she comes home at tea-time."

"I'd no idea that Simon Prentis had a family; hence my curiosity."

"Oh, there's quite a lot of us one way and another. Now perhaps you'd like to see the bedrooms?"

Fenella led the way upstairs. As she had said, the house was very small although particularly charming. Nearly all the bedroom ceilings were sloping, the small-paned windows opening outwards under the gables which gave the house its name.

In the front of the house there was Simon Prentis' room, far the largest and most luxurious of the bed-rooms with a bathroom opening out of it.

There were also two others, smaller and inexpensively furnished, one used by Fenella and the other by her sister. At the back there were the two nurseries and a small bedroom decorated with photographs of football and cricket teams.

"This is my brother Raymond's room," Fenella announced. "He's at sea, so I suppose that if you must billet someone on us they could sleep here."

"I wonder if Raymond would mind very much if I personally occupied his room?"

"You mean you'd come here yourself?"

"If you will let me."

"You will be very uncomfortable. You realize we've got no servants at all now; there's only Nannie and me to do everything."

"Can't you get any help?"

Fenella shook her head.

"Not locally. You see, they don't approve of us in Creepers; in fact," she added, "if you want the truth I don't suppose it will do your reputation any good to stay in this house."

"I think my reputation will stand it," he replied, and his tone was as serious as hers; "but thank you for thinking of me. I appreciate it."

"I'm only warning you. You don't know this part of the country, I presume."

"Not well; but I expect it's like most other parts of rural England—a bit narrow-minded."

Fenella laughed.

"Just a little, although Simon Prentis and family take a lot of swallowing, you know."

"I thought all artists were allowed any amount of licence."

"Not in Creepers."

They shook hands and Rex Ransome said he would be back later.

●　●　●

"It's no use, Nannie," Fenella said wearily, "they can commandeer the entire house if they want to, and after all, Major Ransome seemed quite a nice man.

"He will only be here for breakfast and dinner and he says he'll send a batman up to do his room."

"This used to be a free country," Nannie grumbled.

"No country's free in war time," Fenella replied.

"That's obvious!" Nannie snapped, taking the hot plates off the range and carrying them into the dining-room.

Fenella smiled a little ruefully to herself as she turned

back towards the oven and drew out the shepherd's pie, now browned crisply.

Few people realized that Simon Prentis had six children. Kay, it was true, his eldest daughter and the only child of his first wife Flavia, did make the most of being Simon Prentis' daughter when she went on the stage and later drifted into the films.

Arline's family—Simon had married her in 1920—were less spectacular, which was not surprising for Arline herself had hated the type of self-assertion which must feed its vanity on newspaper cuttings and photographs in the illustrated Press.

The daughter of a respectable and wealthy Scottish family, she had defied her parents when she was only nineteen when they refused to allow her to marry a man who was noted for his Bohemian, unconventional ways.

Surprisingly enough they had been extremely happy. Arline, for all her youth and inexperience, was a strangely sensible and self-sufficient young woman.

She was content to accept Simon as he was, trying neither to change nor convert him to more conventional standards. If he was unfaithful to her during the twelve years of their married life she never showed by word or deed that she was aware of it.

Arline had few friends and had no confidantes, but there were some wise people who wondered just how much of his success Simon owed to her.

For it was Arline who had the practical brain, who remembered to despatch the paintings once they were finished, who kept Simon in touch with the right critics and the important exhibitions.

Yet when she died the vast public who adored Simon and who ate up every detail of his exotic Bohemianism hardly gave a thought to the passing of his wife.

Arline died when Moo was born. It was an unnecessary death brought on by sheer carelessness, by Simon insisting that they left their return from the Continent until the last moment, by crossing the Channel in a violent storm and without bothering to reserve a cabin.

When Arline arrived back at their house in London

15

and Simon handed her over to Nannie, she had already crossed the danger line. Pneumonia set in; Moo arrived with much unnecessary pain and difficulty, and Arline released her never very strong hold on life.

It was doubtful if Simon realized at first what had happened to him. He was distraught with a grief which seemed slightly exaggerated and theatrical.

But it was a selfish grief and he showed it when he enquired of all and sundry what he, Simon Prentis, was going to do with four children on his hands, all of whom except perhaps the eldest were quite incapable of looking after themselves.

Kay by this time was just leaving school, but she had spent most of her childhood with her mother's relations, somewhat flashy surburban people of whom Arline had never approved.

Simon did not really consider her one of his difficulties; but Raymond of eleven, Fenella aged seven, and a baby a month old certainly had to be considered.

It was Nannie who took charge of the household then and who told Simon that London was no place for 'the poor motherless lambs' who wanted a breath of 'God's good air' if they were to be brought up healthy and strong.

At Four Gables the children knew nothing and heard less of what was happening in the great world outside. All they knew of their Father was that he would appear suddenly like a typhoon, sweep into the house, galvanize the whole place into noisy, tempestuous action.

Then he would go as suddenly as he had come, leaving a strange calm and quiet behind, so that they were not certain whether they missed him or were merely relieved at his absence.

It was difficult indeed for them to form an independent opinion, for Nannie made no bones about her feeling in the matter.

Once, half seriously, half laughingly, Simon accused her deliberately of putting the children against their Father. Nannie had faced him defiantly.

16

"I'll lead no child in my charge into the devil's ways," she said.

"So that's what you think of me," Simon had challenged her.

"I was never good at lying," Nannie retorted sturdily.

As Fenella grew older she began to resemble very closely her dead mother. Simon often felt a strange pang as he came upon her suddenly or watched her walk into the room.

Only one thing was lacking—her hair was dark, not red, and being Simon it was impossible for him to admire or find real beauty save in a red-haired woman.

Moo also was dark, but she had a very different type of looks from her elder sister. From the moment she was born Moo had been what Nannie called 'a picture-book baby'.

As Raymond said once:

"Moo is exactly like a box of chocolates, large, succulent, soft-centred ones, tied up with the thickest and most glossy satin ribbon."

Nobody could help liking Moo and she was as pleased as a small friendly puppy with the attention she received.

The arrival of Timothy and Susan after their Father had married Inez in 1936 had really made very little difference. Simon Prentis' marriage had meant just nothing to his children.

There had been so many women after Arline's death in and out of his life that one more or less couldn't be expected to stir them, even though he put a gold ring on her third finger.

The county were slightly scandalized, of course, at what they heard about Simon Prentis, but he certainly had a name and they were prepared to forgive him a good deal because he was reputedly a genius.

But their tentative gestures of friendship were stillborn from the moment Simon Prentis came to Four Gables to live. The stories which were told about him after he arrived were, of course, incredible, fantastic and malicious.

17

A great many had no foundation in fact; but many, unfortunately, were true.

One which never failed to be related with bated breath to every newcomer who had not heard it before, was when a local dignitary, Lady Coleby, an elderly woman who owned the neighbouring estate and was undoubtedly one of the most important people in the district, went to call.

She had been shown by an inexperienced maidservant straight into the barn where Simon was at work.

As usual most of the household were with him. Raymond and Fenella were playing table tennis in a corner of the big room, Moo was singing to her dolls and accompanying herself by strumming on a toy piano.

Simon was standing back from his easel when the visitor was shown in, the maid merely making from the doorway a mumbled sound which nobody heard.

He had half turned towards the newcomer and there was no doubt that she must have felt a quick gasp of admiration, and perhaps even coquetry was not wholly lost in that withered bosom.

At any rate, she had moved forward with a sweeter smile than was usually seen on her narrow, straightened lips. Then, as she held out her hand, an astounding thing happened.

Simon had swooped towards her, taking her arm in his firm grasp and pushing her a few steps to the right.

"Tell me," he had shouted, "tell me what you think? Is that shadow under the left breast green or purple? I've painted it green, but don't hesitate to say if you think I'm wrong."

The startled visitor, conscious of being hurried across a slippery floor, bewildered, yet undeniably aware of the proximity and grip of this giant-like Adonis, had looked with widening eyes across the room to where on the model throne Inez reclined.

Lady Coleby was not to know that she was Simon's wife, although if she had it would have made little difference.

All she was aware of in that horrifying, breathless

18

moment was that she was staring at the recumbent naked body of a young woman posed on a divan of purple plush across which was thrown a Spanish shawl.

Everyone in the painting world was to exclaim later at the daring of the picture—an indescribable riot of colour which no other painter would have ventured to use with a red-haired model.

It had been a much-criticized painting, but not from the angle that the county considered it—that had been something entirely different, for the question of morals had superseded all thought of whether purple plush and crimson flowers were legitimate against the red of a girl's glowing hair.

That incident, alas! had of course prevented a large number of people from calling at Four Gables, but the few who did go out of curiosity had found Simon's indifference to their condescension almost more difficult to accept than his morals.

While the county might eventually have accepted Simon, they would never have accepted Inez, not—as Raymond put it—"in a million years."

She was beautiful, there was no denying that, but she had only to open her mouth for her accent to betray her and the empty banality of her mind to appal those who had been expecting at least something amusing.

Why Simon had married her remained a mystery until Timothy was born five months after the ceremony had taken place, and then a number of people pitied Simon because 'he had done the right thing'.

The marriage was doomed to failure from the beginning; in fact after Timothy arrived they each led their own lives until the war and the imminent danger of air raids frightened Inez into leaving London and taking up her residence at Four Gables.

Simon's desire then to go into the Services, to do his bit to the best of his ability, brought them together for a fleeting and not very convincing reunion.

Susan was born in 1940, and immediately she was about again Inez announced that she had had an offer of a film contract in Hollywood.

A year later she wrote to Simon to say she was divorcing him in Reno as there was someone she particularly wanted to marry. The divorce would not be valid in the United Kingdom, but she thought it was unlikely she would ever return.

She wished him the best of luck and sent her love to the children.

But Fenella wasn't thinking of Simon as she carried the shepherd's pie from the kitchen into the dining-room.

The children were waiting, their bibs tied round their necks, Susan in her high chair next to Nannie who sat at one end of the table while Fenella sat at the other.

She put the dish down on the table and was just going to take her place when she heard the front door-bell ring.

It rang insistently and loudly, as if someone had tugged imperiously and with an unusual strength at the long chain which hung from the lintel down beside the warm old red brick of the wall.

"I wonder who that is?" Fenella said, looking at Nannie.

"I'll go, dearie," Nannie said, half raising in her chair.

It was then Fenella heard Simon's voice calling her name so that it echoed along the passage and seemed to fill the low-ceilinged dining-room.

"Fenella! Fenella! Where are you?"

Everything in the small hall with its low, oak-beamed ceiling was dwarfed in comparison with Simon Prentis.

In his blue Air Force uniform he looked a giant and his vivid colouring was intensified so that he stood out with an almost poster-like flamboyance against the simple cottage surroundings.

Fenella, hurrying forward to kiss her Father, noticed that he was not alone, and with a sinking in her heart took stock of the stranger he had brought with him.

'The usual type!' she thought, then added: 'A little older than most.'

"How are you, my dear?" Simon asked her.

20

He accompanied his kiss with an ardent smack on her behind; then throwing his cap and heavy overcoat down on a chair he inquired:

"Well, what about lunch?"

"But, Daddy," Fenella exclaimed in dismay, "you never let me know you were coming!"

"Didn't let you know! Of course I did," Simon Prentis retorted. "I sent you a wire—at least, I gave one to my secretary. Don't say she forgot!"

"Now did you give it to her, Daddy?" Fenella asked. "Or did you merely think of doing so?"

Simon ran his fingers through his hair.

"Damn it, I believe I did forget!"

"You're hopeless," Fenella said, with the air of one stating a fact rather than making an accusation.

She turned towards the newcomer.

"I'm afraid we're not giving you a very enthusiastic welcome."

"Elaine, this is my daughter Fenella," Simon said simply.

Fenella, taking a soft, rather limp hand in hers, thought:

'I dislike her—I wonder why?'

Elaine—whoever she was—was certainly very attractive. Her vivid red hair, cut page-boy style, was offset by a jaunty black velvet tam-o'-shanter.

She was fashionably thin and her tightly fitting black coat and skirt accentuated the fact. She had, too, Fenella noted swiftly, the type of face which most artists admire—pronounced features with the heavily moulded eyes and rather prominent lips.

"You'd better make a cocktail, Daddy," Fenella said, "while I see what I can find you for lunch. The children are having shepherd's pie, but I don't suppose you'd like that."

"God forbid!" Simon Prentis ejaculated piously.

"Well, I'll go and look in the larder, but I can't promise miracles, so don't expect them."

"I want to wash first," Elaine answered.

21

"I'll show you the bathroom," Fenella said. "Will you come upstairs?"

She led the way while Elaine followed behind her in what Fenella sensed was a sulky silence.

'I wonder who she is?' Fenella mused. 'I hope Simon paints her, because we need some money badly.'

"I'm afraid you'll have to sleep in my room," she said aloud as they reached the door of her bedroom. "I'll move my things immediately after lunch. We're rather cramped here and although the house looks big it's really inconveniently small."

Elained moved disdainfully towards the looking-glass set on the plain oak dressing-table.

"Do you live here all the time?" she asked. "It must be pretty deadly for you."

"I'm used to it," Fenella answered; "but I'm afraid you'll find it rather quiet."

She went out of the room and shut the door behind her.

'She's one of the worst,' she thought as she went downstairs. 'I hope Daddy hasn't got a long leave. This sort of thing is really awfully bad for Moo.'

She hurried into the kitchen and going to the store cupboard took a precious tin of tongue from her invasion store on the top shelf. It took her a few minutes to make a salad to go with it.

Luckily, Nannie had already grated some carrots for the children and she used these, adding beetroot and chopped cabbage heart until the dish looked quite attractive.

There were three eggs which she had collected from the fowls early that morning and these she made into a small omelette, adding some cheese and herbs in the way that she knew her Father liked best.

She ran along the passage to the barn. Simon and Elaine were sipping their cocktails in front of the fire which had just been lit.

"Luncheon's ready, such as it is," Fenella announced gaily, "and do hurry because you've got an omelette and it will spoil if you keep it waiting too long."

Simon was in good spirits, Fenella thought as she watched him walk towards the dining-room humming to himself, moving with that particularly buoyant lilt in his step which was characteristic of him.

While they were eating she put the coffee on to boil and carried upstairs the suitcases which had been left in the hall. She noted that Elaine's was of expensive leather, her initials stamped on it in gold.

When the coffee was ready she carried it into the studio, arranging it on a small table by the fire. As she had expected, as soon as her Father had drunk a cup he announced that he was going to change.

Fenella gave her Father five minutes upstairs alone, then she knocked on his bedroom door.

"Come in," he said.

As she entered he remarked: "Oh, it's you!" with a note of surprise as though he had expected someone else.

"Can you bear to talk business for a moment?" Fenella asked.

"No, I can't," Simon replied; "and if you are going to ask for money, my girl, you can save your breath."

"But, Daddy, I've got to have some."

Simon wrinkled his brow and looked at her.

"This Daddy business is rather overdone," he said unexpectedly. "It makes me feel a hundred and eighty at least. What about being modern and calling me Simon? That goes for Moo, too."

"It sounds so unnatural," Fenella protested. "We always have called you Daddy."

"I know, I know, but it makes me feel damned old. I don't like it."

"I don't think you need worry about getting old," Fenella said with a smile. "Besides, it doesn't matter for a man."

"Yes, it does," Simon retorted.

"All right then—Simon, but if I do this for you I expect you to do something for me and that is to write me a cheque at once."

"But I can't, Fenella; it's no use nagging me."

23

"Now look here," Fenella said, "we can't live on air and you haven't sent me any money for nearly four months—what's more, you haven't answered any of the letters I've written to you about it."

"I know, I know," Simon answered testily; "but I haven't got the money."

He shouted the last words at her.

Fenella walked across to the window and looked out. It was always disturbing when her Father shouted at her. It was silly of her to mind because she knew he meant nothing by it.

Yet she knew that she must hold her ground, and after a moment she turned away from the window to face him, resolution written clearly in the expression on her small face

"I'm sorry," she said quietly, "but you've got to listen to me. We owe nearly two hundred pounds in the neighborhood.

"People round here don't like us—no one knows that better than you. What's more they always have been, always will be, distrustful of artists; they think they are improvident and they are not far wrong.

"Moo's school fees haven't been paid; and as for Nannie, she hasn't had any wages for a long time. The children need new clothes—I can't get those on credit because we haven't got accounts at the London shops at the moment. "That is the position, Simon, and you've got to face it."

Simon looked across the room at her, opened his mouth to bellow, then changed his mind and said nothing.

Fenella thankful for his restraint, had no idea that it was due to the fact that at that moment she looked so exactly like her mother as to hurt Simon with an almost unbearable sense of loss.

That was how Arline had spoken when she had meant to get something—quietly, clearly, but with an unmistakable Scottish determination which kept her unswervingly to the point however hard her husband might try to prevaricate or evade it.

"There's only one thing to do," he said, standing up, "I must start painting at once. Boggis has been worrying me for a picture for months and months. Well, I'll give him one and that should set us on our feet for a bit."

"If you will start it right away," Fenella said, "I will telephone Mr. Boggis and I know he'll give me an advance on it."

"Give you an advance?" Simon asked, half angrily. "Who's painting this picture?"

"You are," Fenella replied, "and if you don't hurry over it the Prentis family will be begging their bread from door to door—and that won't do your publicity any good."

"Damn you, you're a slave driver!" Simon shouted, but he caught his daughter round the shoulders and gave her a bear-like hug. "I'm the worst Father in Christendom.

"Nannie's right in all she's ever said about me, but I'll turn over a new leaf right away, although I don't suppose this change of heart will last long."

He laughed at his own inconstancy, then he went downstairs whistling cheerily, leaving Fenella to pick up his clothes which had been scattered negligently on the floor and on the bed and put them away in the wardrobe.

Downstairs, Elaine pouted petulantly when Simon told her that he wanted her to model for his latest picture.

At the same time she was secretly delighted; all through her short, but ardent love affair with the handsome Simon she had been hoping he would suggest painting her and had been slightly piqued when the invitation had not been forthcoming.

The publicity and fame which was always the perquisite of Simon's models was payment enough for the boredom and weariness of the sittings.

"I've got the very dress upstairs in my box," she said. "It's a white chiffon. Why don't you do an all-white picture, Simon?—it would be original."

"Original!" Simon snorted. "It's what every would-

25

be portrait painter does in his second year at an art school. For goodness sake, woman, talk of things you know about, not of art which you know nothing. Now let me see."

He walked up and down the studio rubbing his hands and fingers through his hair.

"You're much too thin to be done naked unless I want to give the public a lesson in anatomy."

"Don't be so ridiculous, Simon," Elaine said furiously. "I've got a wonderful figure—everybody says so."

"You've got a fashionable figure, my dear. That's a very different thing. To me you appear to be giving an impersonation of life in the occupied countries."

"If you go on like this," Elaine pouted, "I shan't sit for you at all."

"Oh yes you will," Simon replied. "You're delighted to do so and don't I know it. It's not every woman who loves Simon Prentis who has the opportunity to model for him, I can promise you that."

"I think you are detestable and unbearably conceited."

"Why shouldn't I be?" Simon asked. "Is there anyone to touch me in the art world at the moment? You know there isn't. And there's no one, my dear little fool, who can make you as famous as I am going to make you and well you know it. Come here. Sit on that chair and let's see how you look."

He posed her in various positions, unsatisfied and critical until she got really exasperated with him.

"Go and put your white dress on, then," he said at length. "I expect I shall loathe it, but I'm damned if I paint that coat and skirt. I always did hate red-heads in black—it's too obvious."

Elaine went upstairs while Simon got out his paints and brushes, happy because he had been driven to work.

It was nearly twenty minutes before Elaine reappeared. She had taken as much trouble with her appearance as if she were going to be photographed.

Her white dress was, as she had promised Simon,

particularly attractive, the chiffon was swathed about her and had been cut with a cunning which could be achieved only by a French dressmaker.

Her red hair, brushed until it was shining with the dark burnished sheen of polished brass, touched the white nakedness of her shoulders, and her arms glittered with diamond bracelets.

"Ready for the Court Ball, I see," Simon said mockingly with a bow.

"Now do you understand what I mean?" Elaine asked. "A white background with my hair the only touch of colour—oh, Simon, it would be divine!"

"It would," Simon said grimly. "They would doubtless buy up the copyright at Woolworth's and sell them at sixpence a copy entitled 'Snow White'."

"I think you're beastly. I shan't offer you any more of my ideas."

She moved across the room gracefully, then stopped before a small mirror hanging on the wall and peered into it.

"I've got it!" Simon shouted.

"Got what?" Elaine asked.

There was no need for Simon to answer, he was pulling the chairs and things he had arranged on the model throne off on to floor.

Then he lifted up a table and chair, both rather severe in their period perfection, and going to the door shouted for Fenella.

"Fenella! Fenella!"

His voice rang out penetrating the furthest corners of the house.

Fenella came running down the stairs. She had been helping Nannie get the children ready for their walk and wondered from the urgency of her Father's voice what had happened.

"What is it, Dad . . I mean Simon?"

"I want that three-sided mirror in your bedroom," he said. "You know the one I mean."

"It's the one Elaine will be using," Fenella said warningly.

She knew that once Simon was using something in his studio it wouldn't be allowed to be moved until he had finished with it.

"What the devil does that matter?" he asked. "Go and get it."

She did as she was told, wondering where she and Moo would get a looking-glass after they had given up theirs to Elaine.

She came down the stairs staggering under the weight of the glass. It was quite a cheap one, framed in gilded wood, but attractive, with the carved figures of two small cupids on the top of the centre mirror.

"That's the one I want," Simon said with satisfaction.

He put it on the table he had arranged; then, sitting Elaine on the chair, told her to put one elbow on the table and look into the mirror.

"You ought to enjoy this," he remarked. "You'll be able to stare at your own face the whole time."

"I must say it's the one thing that's least likely to bore me in this place," Elaine retorted.

It took some time for Simon to pose her; then at last he was satisfied and turned towards his easel.

"Don't go away," he said to Fenella, who was watching. "I shall want your advice. Do you see my idea?"

She looked at Elaine from the angle at which he stood and realized that it was a clever position.

One could see Elaine almost full-face within the centre mirror and could also catch a glimpse of her profile in both the side glasses.

"Haven't you made her sit in rather a drooping fashion?" Fenella asked.

"I want her like that," Simon said, "and look—pull that shoulder strap off her left shoulder."

Fenella moved across the room, yet somehow when she reached Elaine she disliked touching the woman. She was not sure why; but as she did as her Father had commanded she felt a sudden shudder of distaste as her fingers touched the cool white flesh.

She moved away thinking that the picture would look somewhat abandoned, but knowing that Simon would

28

have some reason for the arrangement. He always saw a picture as a subject rather than a portrait.

She was still worrying over finance when the front doorbell rang. She hurriedly went to answer it.

On the doorstep was standing a nice-looking young man of about twenty-five. Fenella recognized him at once; he was Sir Nicholas Coleby, their near neighbour at Wetherby Court.

"I'm sorry to bother you," Sir Nicholas said, "but is Major Ransome here?"

He spoke with a suspicion of a stammer in his voice, and Fenella saw, too, that he was walking with a stick. It was the first time for two years that Sir Nicholas had been off crutches.

He had been wounded in the Battle of Britain and prayers had been offered over the whole county for his recovery. That he had recovered at all was due to his youth and to the amazing strides surgery had made since the last war.

He looked pale, there were dark lines under his eyes, but he was a very different person from the wreck of a man who had been brought in an ambulance back to his home after six months in hospital.

"I'm afraid Major Ransom isn't here at the moment."

Fenella had never spoken to Sir Nicholas Coleby before and she noted that his voice was low and his manner almost boyishly shy as if he was embarrassed at having to come to the house.

'It must be rather difficult for him,' she thought to herself, 'knowing what his mother thinks of us.'

"They told me at the camp that he might be here," Sir Nicholas insisted.

"He came here before luncheon," Fenella said, "and he is coming back in time for dinner. That is all I know about his movements, I'm afraid."

Sir Nicholas hesitated.

"It is rather important for me to see him," he said at length. "Would it be very inconvenient if I called in for a moment after dinner? I'd telephone, only something's gone wrong with ours—I think it was the storm last night—anyway, it isn't in working order yet."

"It will be perfectly all right for you to come back later," Fenella said.

"Thank you very much."

He raised his hat, turned and hobbled down the steps to where a car awaited him. He got into it with difficulty.

Having lowered himself cautiously and carefully into the driving-seat, he looked up to see Fenella still waiting on the steps and raised his hat once again before he drove off.

'He seems rather nice,' Fenella thought as she went back into the house. 'I wonder if his mother knows he's been here. I don't suppose she'd be best pleased.'

It was well known that Lady Coleby ruled her son and, indeed, her whole household with a rod of iron.

When she had banned the Prentis household as immoral and unknowable there were few people brave enough to dare her wrath and call.

The villagers, too, had taken their tone from her and Fenella knew that because Lady Coleby spoke openly of her dislike and distrust of the family at Four Gables she was often treated casually, if not rudely, when she went shopping in Creepers.

CHAPTER TWO

During the afternoon Rex Ransome had found his thoughts turning continually towards the Prentis family and in particular Fenella.

He had been obliged to drive some twenty miles to his headquarters in another county; but all the time he was journeying there and back he found himself thinking of a small, pointed face with large dark eyes.

'Simon Prentis . . Simon Prentis . .'

Rex Ransome repeated the name over and over to himself as he tried to remember more clearly the gossip and chatter of the past.

Snatches of it came back to him, but the whole picture of the man remained intangible in his mind.

He could remember his paintings, of course—they were unforgettable and far too famous to be forgotten.

From the point of view of the popular Press Simon Prentis had made his name by his daring, suggestive pictures of red-headed women; but the world who understood art knew him as a painter of genius, capable of portraying many different aspects of life.

His still-life studies, for instance, Rex Ransome could remember one—a breakfast table in Paris set before a window through which one could see the house opposite and the first pale glimmer of spring sunshine; the effect of light and shade had been amazing.

There was another, too, which he could remember very clearly—a monastery gateway painted at midday; the effect of sunlight on the grey stone, which even when bathed by light and warmth seemed to retain the austerity and the frigid chill of age and isolation, had been symbolic.

There was no doubt the man was one of the brilliant personalities of the century and Rex Ransome hoped he would meet him.

For one thing, he would like to know the real meaning of the picture he himself possessed. What was it that had made the woman laugh?

Despite his anxiety to get away from camp and back to Four Gables, Rex was kept later than usual. There were a great many things to be seen to and the places where he had been able to billet his men were not entirely satisfactory.

However, at last he found himself driving up the long, unkempt drive which led to Four Gables.

The house itself stood on the top of a hill overlooking the village and was sheltered at the back by a thick belt of trees, part of the extensive woodlands which stretched for miles and almost entirely surrounded Wetherby Court, Sir Nicholas Coleby's place.

He switched off the engine and lifted out his suitcases.

He had meant to bring his batman with him, but it was the man's supper-time and he had arranged for him to bicycle up afterwards and do what unpacking there was to be done.

"You'll have to make yourself useful in lots of ways," Rex had told him. "They've got no help in the house and it's rather an imposition my having to billet myself on the ladies anyway."

He fancied that he had detected an expression of resentment in the man's eyes, but he couldn't be quite sure.

'Lazy devil!' he thought. 'It won't hurt him for once to do a little extra—they have an easy enough life.'

He well knew that he was noted for driving his men

hard, but it was no harder than he drove himself; in fact, of the two, his was the worst.

At times Rex Ransome's brother officers wondered what it was that galvanized him into such unremitting action; he seemed to glory in making work and in finding it even when on the surface it appeared unnecessary.

What was more, he seldom went on leave, although he was comparatively lenient in granting it to others.

"Strange chap!" was the general verdict amongst those who shared the Mess with him. "One can't help liking him and yet one never gets to know him well. He's as much a stranger at the end of six months as he is during the first six days."

If Rex knew what was said about him he showed no signs of wishing to increase his intimate friends or of making a bid for cheap popularity.

He was, it is true, intensely reserved and he seemed a little withdrawn from the officers under him so that they treated him with a somewhat frigid respect, seldom including him in their jokes or in their more intimate conversations.

One characteristic was his loathing of parties of any sort; he would never accept an invitation to one if he could possibly help it.

It was well known that if there was a chance for him to be absent on a guest night without being obviously rude, he would always take it.

It was with a quick frown of repugnance that Rex, stepping into the hall of Four Gables, heard the noise of voices and laughter coming from the big room which Fenella had told him was her father's studio.

He had somehow looked forward to finding Fenella alone and having a quiet evening talking to her, getting to know her better; but now as he stood hesitating in the dimness of the hall, the door of the studio was flung open and one of the prettiest young girls he had ever seen came running out, almost charging into him before she noticed his presence.

"Oh, gracious!" she exclaimed.

Then the surprise faded from her face and she held out her hand.

"I expect it's Major Ransome, isn't it?" she asked. "Fenella told us you were coming. I'm Moo."

Her smile was friendly and welcoming, but Rex could only stare at her as he took the hand she offered.

He had not expected anything quite so exquisitely lovely as this. She was only a child, of course, and too fat as yet—puppy fat.

She'd fine down later and then, he thought, be almost breath-taking in a rather obviously beautiful manner.

"Won't you come in?" Moo asked. "I was just going to fetch some glasses. Daddy's making one of his extra special cocktails."

"Your Father's home?" Rex asked.

Moo nodded.

"Arrived at lunch-time unexpectedly. Come on—come and be introduced."

She led him into the studio even as another shout of laughter—deep, full-throated laughter—came bursting towards them in an overwhelming wave of sound.

Simon was standing in front of the fire-place, his legs apart, a bottle of gin in one hand, a cocktail shaker in the other.

He was wearing a plum-coloured smoking-jacket, exquisitely cut, which showed off his wide shoulders and was with its satin lapels in pleasing contrast to the golden tone of his skin.

Something had amused him and he had flung back his head, bellowing out his laughter.

Immediately he entered the room Rex was conscious that Fenella was there. She was sitting on the arm of a chair by the fireside and she was looking up at her Father with an inscrutable expression on her face which Rex could not fathom.

Then even as he advanced towards Simon Prentis and the painter's great hand went out in welcome, he saw the woman who had been sitting with her back to the door—sitting staring at Simon Prentis with her red lips parted, her thin hands clasped round her knees as if in ecstasy.

"How do you do, Major," Simon was saying. "My daughter tells me that you are honouring our humble abode. We are only too pleased, of course, to offer what we can—but that's not saying much."

"Rex, this is a surprise!"

Rex forced himself to turn in the direction of the slow, artificial tones.

"How are you, Elaine?"

He wondered if anyone in the room noticed that he made no attempt to shake hands with her.

"Need you ask? I'm always well and generally managing to enjoy myself."

There was a defiant note in her voice—it was as if she issued him a challenge.

"You know each other, then?" Simon asked.

"We do."

Rex spoke grimly, but Elaine, moving across to Simon, linked her arm through his.

"Simon darling," she said, "who was the person who made that excruciating remark about the world being so small? He was right..

"If I was never certain of it before I am now, for you see Rex and I are very old friends—and very old enemies, in fact the last time we met he expressed a pious desire that he might never see me again."

"Well, his prayer obviously hasn't been answered," Simon said; "but knowing you, I expect he had a good reason for uttering it!"

Elaine laughed, a sound which had little humour in it.

"He thought he had," she said with an accent on the verb. "You see, he'd just informed me that he intended to divorce me."

If Rex Ransome was embarrassed he showed no sign of it.

"I don't think our private affairs are of particular interest to other people, Elaine," he said. "Besides, it's an

35

old story. If you will excuse me, sir, I'd like to wash before dinner."

"Of course," Simon replied. "Do you know the way? There's no need to go upstairs, you'll find a cloakroom just by the front door."

"Thank you."

Rex left the room, walking smoothly and with an unhurried gait. As he went, he heard Elaine laugh on a shrill note with a touch of hysteria in it.

"Good Lord, Elaine!" Simon Prentis said to her. "Do we need to come all the way to the country to pick up bits of your past?"

"It appears so," Elaine answered. "Really, Simon, this is the last place I should have expected to find Rex. I thought he was still abroad. He had a farm in Kenya for some time."

"Well, he's certainly back now," Simon ejaculated, "and staying in my house. You see, Fenella, what comes of trying to do your duty to your King and Country."

"I'll go and see about dinner," Fenella said. "Don't make me a cocktail; I don't want one."

She, too, left the room, and when she had gone Elaine stared after her before she turned to Simon with something suspiciously like a sneer.

"I don't think your daughter's particularly friendly to me, Simon."

"Why should she be?" Simon asked. "I didn't bring you here to be a companion for her."

There was something in his tone of voice which told Elaine it would be wise to drop the conversation.

He slapped her gently on her cheek and turned away. She felt discomforted, more unsure of him at that moment than ever before; but before she could speak Moo came through the door carrying the glasses and Rex was behind her.

"Here we are," Moo said. "I'm sorry to have been so long, but I could only find three."

"Will you have a cocktail, Ransome?" Simon Prentis asked.

"Thank you."

He took the glass which Simon offered him and carried it across the fire-place to Elaine.

"Allow me," he said with a kind of mocking politeness.

For a moment there was hostility in her expression and then suddenly Elaine smiled.

"Thank you, Rex. It's quite like old times to have you waiting on me."

"You always enjoyed being waited on, Elaine," he replied.

She noted there was no bitterness in his tone, only a quiet amusement, and it annoyed her more than any antagonism would have done.

There was something almost unbearable in seeing Rex after all these years so detached, so sure of himself, so—yes, inscrutable was the word she wanted.

What is he thinking? she wondered.

Did he remember that wild, mad scene when he had discovered her infidelity? She had thought then that her last moment had come; she had believed that Rex meant to kill her.

When finally he had left her she had realized that she had experienced stark physical fear—the fear of being murdered, of being killed by the man who had loved her too much.

How strange it all seemed now and what a fool she had been to let Rex find out. She had lost a great deal in losing him.

He had been rich, for one thing, and she had known moments of poverty in the years that followed their divorce, moments which left her increasingly afraid each time of what the future would hold for her if her looks faded.

● ● ●

"Sir Nicholas is nice—I do like him!"

Moo was sitting up in bed, watching Fenella while she undressed, and looking for all the world like an American advertisement for some special make of mattress or bed linen.

37

The white pillows were a perfect background for her vivid colouring, and the soft blue of her nightgown, old though it was and washed many times, showed off the whiteness of her skin and the soft, tender curves of a young body nearing adolescence.

"He seemed very shy," Fenella said, "but then I expect he felt embarrassed. It must be rather an ordeal to be pitchforked into our family."

Moo laughed.

"I really felt quite sorry for him when Major Ransome remarked, 'Of course you know everyone here', and he had to admit that he didn't know a soul."

"Poor Sir Nicholas!" Fenella exclaimed; "I'm sure he's more sinned against than sinning. Everyone says he hasn't a chance even of expressing an opinion when his mother's around."

"I wonder if he'll tell her he's been here."

"I've a feeling he won't."

Fenella got up from the dressing-table, turned out the lights, opened wide the windows, then groping her way across the darkened room got into bed.

"It's awfully late," she said. "You'll be dead tired to-morrow, Moo."

"I don't care," Moo replied. "I haven't enjoyed myself so much for a long time and oh!—there's so much I want to ask you."

"Keep it for to-morrow," Fenella cautioned. "I'm going to sleep. Good night, darling."

"Good night, Fenella."

Moo turned over restlessly two or three times and then Fenella heard her even breathing and knew she had fallen asleep as easily and quickly as an over-tired child.

Despite her good resolution she herself could not sleep. She lay thinking, recalling the many events that had taken place that day.

She found herself going over the conversation word for word, recapturing that moment when she had found Major Ransome standing on the doorstep, when she had heard her Father's voice bellowing out the announcement of his arrival.

And when she had first seen Elaine, beautiful, sophisticated and yet somehow definitely antagonistic. It seemed unreal that she and Rex Ransome should have been married.

What a ridiculous coincidence that they should meet so unexpectedly and in a way so dramatically!

Did Rex Ransome mind about Simon? Fenella wondered, and knew the answer even while she asked the question. No one could have been more at ease than he had been during the evening.

At first she had expected him to be difficult to talk to; he had a reserved, almost repressive air about him, but at dinner he had changed completely.

He had kept them all laughing, even Elaine had joined in reluctantly although every now and then she had tried to hurt him with some barbed sentence containing an intimate meaning known only to themselves.

But instinctively Fenella had known that Elaine had not hurt the man who had once been her husband.

She thought back over Simon's past—the young, the ardent and the passionate red-heads who had come and gone.

It was funny, Fenella thought, how unimportant they had been.

It was difficult now to remember anything about them, even their names; they were just a kaleidoscope of red hair and artificially darkened eyelashes, of crimson lips and white skins, of features which were infinitely more expressive on canvas than in real life.

The critics said that Simon always glamorized his models; one thing was quite certain—he gave them far more personality in paint than they ever possessed in the flesh.

But somehow Elaine was different, Fenella sensed that even after so short an acquaintance, and yet she wondered whether she would have found her different had it not been for the added complication of having Rex Ransome in the house.

"I like him," she told herself.

She felt unexpectedly a sudden warmth at the remembrance of the way he had smiled at her, the things he had said during the evening which had been meant for her ear alone.

Little things, trivial things, so unimportant that it seemed surprising that she should remember every one of them; every word and every intonation of his voice as he said them.

Yet she could remember, could still feel the touch of his hand, hard, firm and strong as he had wished her good night.

'He's kind, too,' Fenella thought.

She remembered how he had put young Sir Nicholas Coleby at his ease.

Moo was right, it had been awkward for the young man coming in on them like that.

He had called as he had promised, but they had been making so much noise in the studio that they had not heard the front door-bell.

In fact Sir Nicholas must have waited some time before Nannie, irritable at being disturbed, had come slowly down from the nurseries to open the door to him.

She had asked Sir Nicholas in, left him standing in the hall while in her usual abrupt manner she had opened the door of the studio and remarked tersely:

"Someone to see Major Ransome."

It was Fenella who had remembered who it was.

"I'm so sorry, Major," she had said, "but I forgot to tell you Sir Nicholas Coleby called here this afternoon. He wants particularly to see you and he said he'd come back again this evening."

"Oh, I know what it's about," Rex Ransome said, rising; "I'm sorry he should have the journey twice."

He got up and walked towards the door.

"Do take him into the little sitting-room," Fenella had called after him.

But he could not have heard her for a moment or so later he had brought Sir Nicholas into the studio.

Fenella wondered what the young man must have

thought as he walked into the room from which his mother had fled in disgust years before, never to return.

'I am sure this is what he expected to find,' she thought, looking at Elaine, who was still wearing the white décolleté dress in which Simon was painting her and was holding cupped in her hands to warm it a huge brandy glass.

Simon had been arguing a point of anatomy and some sketches of nudes were strewn over the sofa where he was half lying, half sitting, a cigar between his lips.

'We must look very Bohemian,' Fenella thought, and then realized that Sir Nicholas was staring, not at Elaine or Simon, but at Moo.

'I suppose she is rather breath-taking when one sees her for the first time,' she said to herself, aware that Moo had dressed up that night in honour of Major Ransome.

A strange man at dinner was something of an event at Four Gables. Moo was wearing a picture frock of green velvet which Fenella had made for her out of some curtains which Simon had used in a picture many years ago.

It made her look older and taller than she was and hid a great deal of her plumpness so that she looked particularly alluring.

After the first moment of introduction and the stammered apologies from Sir Nicholas, the awkwardness passed and soon they were all chatting round the fire.

Simon, in one of his good moods when he was glad to have an audience whoever they might be, made no attempt to be provocatively disagreeable, as he often was to local people.

'If only things could always go as well,' Fenella found herself thinking.

She looked at Moo's rapt eagerness and hearing her laughter ring out so spontaneously and happily she felt a sudden pang of pity and anxiety. Poor Moo! She minded ostracism so much.

How happy Moo would have been to be the daughter of respectable country people, to be asked to tea-parties and sewing-bees, to play in the local tennis tournament.

She would have saved up so that she might have a new dress for the Hunt Ball, and would have looked forward with passionate eagerness to one holiday a year at the seaside or some good centre where young people of decent families foregathered.

Moo would have enjoyed every moment of a life like that, asking nothing more than to meet kindness and good humour, to command attention because she was young and not unattractive, to be useful in a small community.

It was so very little to want of life and yet it was the one thing she was never likely to get.

Fenella sighed involuntarily at her thoughts and then she had heard Rex Ransome's voice asking her quietly:

"What's worrying you? Won't you tell me? 'A worry shared,' you know."

Fenella had smiled.

"I was looking into the future."

"Surely a very unwise thing to do?"

"Do you really think that?" Fenella challenged. "I should have thought you would have been intensely practical, the sort of person who planned ahead and took out a life insurance."

"Do I really appear as dull as that?" he had asked, and made her retract her words.

It was Sir Nicholas Coleby who had broken up the party, for that was what it had seemed as they all sat around the fire.

"Please forgive me," he had said in his shy, hesitant way, "but I think I ought to be going home."

"Come in again any time you're passing, my boy," Simon said magnanimously. "We shall always be delighted to see you."

"That's very kind of you, Sir."

"Not at all, I like people round me. The trouble about this part of the world is that it's so damned dull."

"I'm glad you have the decency to admit it," Elaine grumbled.

"There's no reason for you to say that," Simon retorted, "for the very first night you've come to Four Gables we've produced two charming young men for your approval."

"I hardly think Rex qualifies for either adjective," Elaine said, "but Sir Nicholas most certainly."

She held out her hand to the young man, dazzling him with a smile and with a flash of her eyes.

He had shaken hands all round, he had stammered a word of thanks to Fenella, and then Rex Ransome had escorted him to the front door.

"And now we must go to bed," Fenella had said, knowing that for Moo's sake she must be firm.

It was not good for the child to sit up too late, but it was impossible to get away. She had the feeling that Simon really meant his protestations of "Nonsense! I'm not here often, and rules and regulations must be broken for once."

"Well, if you will soothe Nannie down in the morning," Fenella said, "and not be angry if you don't get your breakfast until nearly lunchtime."

"I'll get my own," Simon promised.

Then pretended to be annoyed at their somewhat rude laughter.

"We don't want the house burned down just yet," Moo said. "Do you remember when you left your paintbrushes boiling all night and how angry Nannie was when she found it was the milk saucepan that you'd put them in?"

Rex Ransome came back into the room and sat down in front of the fire.

"That's a decent young chap," he said. "He's given me every facility I could possibly want on his estate and a good deal more than I have asked for."

"I'd love to see Wetherby Court," Moo said unexpectedly. "I believe it's a wonderful house—terribly old."

"Haven't you ever been there?" Rex asked.

"We're not likely to receive an invitation," she said wistfully.

"Why not?" he asked unthinkingly.

Moo had hesitated for a moment, then told the truth.

"Don't you understand. No one knows us round here. Why the girls I go to school with would no sooner ask me back to their homes than fly.

"They wouldn't keep me in the school if I hadn't been there such a long time and, if you ask me, it'll be a red-letter day for them when they can say good-bye to me."

Moo spoke with sudden bitterness which was almost painful. There was a silence, then Simon, getting up from the sofa to stand in front of the fire, said:

"My dear child, if you're going to worry what every congenital half-wit says you're going to be extremely unhappy in your life. You have the privilege—and I mean that—of belonging to an intelligent family. What more can you ask?"

"A good deal," Moo had exclaimed hotly.

Then Fenella had bent forward and put a restraining hand upon Moo's, checking the words which flooded to her lips.

"It's no use, Moo," she said. "Daddy can't help it; whatever you say will only annoy him."

"Don't be so absurd," Simon said. "Why should I be annoyed? Let the child say what she wants."

He was in his most genial mood, but Fenella knew how little it would take to make him furious with anger, to turn his calm benevolence into a fighting fury. She linked her fingers through Moo's, silencing her with their pressure.

"It's nothing, Simon," she said. "It's just a bit dull in this part of the world and occasionally we get fed up. You'd better hurry up and finish the new picture, and perhaps Moo and I will be able to take a trip to London."

● ● ●

Laying in the darkness Fenella wondered about Elaine. She was obviously in love with Simon, and yet while that was nothing new she hoped that Simon was not really interested in her.

During the evening, however, there had been one remark passed which had seemed to Fenella to have a special significance.

While Elaine was moving about the studio one of the bracelets which she wore round her wrist had fallen to the ground. She picked it up with a sharp exclamation of annoyance.

"It's the clasp again, Simon," she said irritably. "I told you it wasn't strong enough, but you wouldn't wait for them to alter it."

It was a lovely bracelet, Fenella had noted, of diamonds and a few small but perfect emeralds set in platinum. For a moment Fenella had been too angry to do anything but walk away to the far end of the room and grapple with her own feelings.

So this was why Simon had sent them no money lately, why they had had the humiliation of asking locally for more and more credit, why Nannie had to do without wages and why they had all had to get along without new clothes, without even buying shoes and stockings which were real necessities where she and Moo were concerned.

For a moment Fenella felt herself quivering, even as Moo had, on the verge of an outburst.

Then something hard and resolute was born within her and the last atom of childish admiration for her Father faded away, making her see him no longer as a kind of god to whom she must offer a somewhat frightened adoration, but as a man.

'I'll make him finish that picture,' Fenella thought, 'and I'll take all the money for the children, every penny of it.'

"There's a row going on," Moo announced, bouncing into the room where Fenella was ironing.

"A row?" Fenella questioned.

"Elaine and Daddy—I beg his pardon, I should have said Simon! Doesn't it seem ridiculous, calling him by his Christian name? I always feel as though I am being impertinent and that any moment Nannie will send me to bed or make me stand in a corner."

45

Fenella put down her iron.

"What do you mean—a row?" she asked.

"Well, I was just going into the studio when I heard them," Moo replied; "in fact, I should think by now you could hear them halfway down the drive. They're going it hammer and tongs!"

Moo spoke with something like relish, but Fenella said in a tone which was meant to be reproving:

"I hope you are wrong."

"I'm not and you know it," Moo retorted, sitting down in the low window-seat and curling her legs under her. "Do you know what I've decided, Fenella?"

"No—what?"

Moo's tone had altered to one of deep seriousness, but Fenella was used to these sudden changes of mood.

"When I grow up," Moo said, "I am going to marry somebody very important and highly respectable—somebody like Nicholas Coleby—and I shall never allow my children to know anything about the more sordid side of life."

Fenella smiled, she couldn't help herself. Moo was given to using rather pompous platitudes as though she herself had originated them.

"I think your ambition is an excellent one."

Moo turned swiftly to look at her.

"And what's more," she said defiantly, "I'll never ask Daddy inside my house—never, never! I shall forget my family except you, Fenella; I'll always love you, of course."

"Thank you very much, but you mayn't approve of me by that time."

"I shall always approve of you," Moo said adoringly; "but Fenella—I'm afraid."

"What of?"

"You'll laugh at me."

"I won't, I promise," Fenella said. " 'Cross my heart'."

It was an old catchword; they had used it for years, brought to the house originally by Raymond.

"Really truly?" Moo asked.

"Really truly," Fenella repeated solemnly.

"Then," Moo said in a low voice, "I'm afraid of being 'bad style'."

It was with difficulty that Fenella could keep her promise not to laugh. Moo looked so desperately serious and it was impossible to think of her being anything but absurdly beautiful, and yet with a pang of pity Fenella knew only too well what she meant.

How many women had she seen in her own home in the last few years who were not 'bad style'? But at school she had learnt to differentiate between them and the mothers and sisters of the other girls.

"I don't think you need worry," Fenella said.

"You don't think our mother was like . ." Moo hesitated, ". . like Elaine and those other women that Simon goes about with now?"

"I know she wasn't. You've only got to look at her photographs and the picture Simon painted of her."

The two girls were silent for a moment, thinking of the picture which they both loved but which Simon could never bear to see.

They had been half afraid at one time that he would sell it, and Inez hated it too, but for a very different reason. So Nannie had taken the portrait and hung it in her own room—the little room up in the attic.

She never slept there now that she was with the children in the night nursery, but it contained all her personal belongings and treasures collected during her years of service.

The door was kept locked, but though they never mentioned it among themselves the children knew that it was locked against their father, just in case in a moment of madness he took that picture away and destroyed it.

It hung there on the only straight wall, dwarfing the room, utterly out of place, for its frame was only a few feet off the ground, but somehow every time they visited the room they felt as if they went to a shrine.

Simon had painted Arline simply and, for him, conventionally. There was no problem, no story behind this

47

picture except his own, for he had painted the woman he loved.

Arline was seated on a grass bank with a rather symbolic-looking tree behind her; there was a suggestion of blue sky, while sunlight flooded the whole picture turning everything to living gold.

She was smiling slightly and her expression was one of deep contentment and happiness.

To her children she had always seemed to be looking straight at them, giving them comfort and understanding and a little of the love they had missed all through the years without her.

She was attractive, there was no mistaking that, but both Fenella and Moo knew there was something else there too—dignity and breeding.

All the things which they would have wanted in their mother and which they knew were lamentably lacking in most of their father's friends.

As if she had followed her sister's thoughts Moo said now:

"Do you think anyone seeing us for the first time, Fenella, and not knowing who we were or anything about us, would think that we were ladies—you and I?"

"I'm quite certain they would," Fenella said firmly.

She was disturbed by the question, worried that Moo should have thought fit to ask it.

She herself had often felt rebellious against their isolation and against the position in which they found themselves in the county, but it had been left to Moo to put her anxiety into words, to express those things which Fenella knew had often disturbed her, but of which she had never spoken.

"I'm glad," Moo said simply.

"But it isn't only what you are born, you know," Fenella went on. "It's what you make yourself."

"You can see that with Elaine, can't you?" Moo said unexpectedly perceptive.

"I suppose you can."

"Well, I don't think she'll be here for long!" Moo said.

Suddenly her seriousness was gone and an impish smile twisted her lips.

"I heard her shouting the most awful words at Daddy. She sounded as if she hated him."

"I hope Simon has finished the picture, then," Fenella remarked, and now she was really anxious.

Mr. Boggis had come down the day before, excited at the thought of handling a picture by Simon after a long and barren interval.

"How you remind me of your mother," he had said to Fenella just before the local taxi arrived to take him back to the station.

"You can't say anything that pleases me more," Fenella remarked, "but why?"

"You're getting her business ability," Mr. Boggis replied. "She always managed the financial side of—well, shall we call it your Father's business?"

"I'll telephone you as soon as the picture is finished," Fenella promised.

"Don't let anyone touch it or move it until I send my men down to pack it up," Mr. Boggis commanded.

"I shall guard it very carefully indeed," Fenella promised; "and, Mr. Boggis—you will send the rest of the money direct to me, won't you?"

"Your Father seemed to agree to that," Mr. Boggis said a little doubtfully. "It's irregular, of course. If you could have got him to sign a letter instructing me to do so I should have felt happier about it."

"Oh, please, Mr. Boggis! You know what Father's like."

"Yes, I do indeed," Mr. Boggis had said.

Fenella fancied that he gave her a compassionate look before he raised his ancient felt hat from his greying head and disappeared into the darkness of the out-of-date taxi.

She was still a little afraid that she might not really get the bulk of the money in the future, but she had got the advance of five hundred pounds.

"Once I get the rest of the money for the picture,"

Fenella said suddenly, "we are going to go away for a holiday, Moo—war or no war."

She spoke optimistically and yet there was a desperate fear within her that the picture would never be finished.

Her anxiety drew Fenella across the room to open the door. She stepped out into the passage, listening, but she could hear nothing.

"They're quiet enough now," she said. "I expect you are exaggerating."

"I'm not, really," Moo retorted. "Elaine was swearing like a trooper. Would you like to hear what she said?"

"I would not," Fenella said decidedly, "and if I were you, I should forget it."

"Oh, she didn't teach me anything new. Don't be so stuffy, Fenella; at times you talk as though you were an aged aunt of sixty-three."

"How do you know what an aged aunt would be like?"

"I've seen lots of women of the type I mean who I'm sure are people's aunts. Have you ever wondered, Fenella, what our own relations are like?"

"Yes, often," Fenella admitted frankly. "But it hasn't got me very far."

"I've a good mind to write and ask them to invite me to stay," Moo said.

"Oh, Moo, you couldn't!" Fenella cried, horrified at the idea. "After all, it would be frightfully disloyal to Daddy. Besides, if they'd really wanted us they'd have made an overture years ago."

"That's just why I haven't done it," Moo said. "I think it was beastly of them not to make any attempt to see us. Well, I suppose they felt that as Mother had made her bed we must all lie on it."

Fenella laughed.

"We're being ridiculous about ourselves. I expect we've all got a complex if we but knew it."

"I don't know," Moo said. "We're not like other people. I'd like to be ordinary like the girls at school.

"You should see the Headmistress when some of the mothers come round; they may be dull and dowdy, but she literally purrs with pleasure, especially to the ones who've got a title."

"Darling, you'll have to marry a duke and then you can open bazaars all day long and everyone will make a fuss of you."

"I'd adore it. And, Fenella—shall I tell you something?"

What Moo was going to say was lost for ever, for at that moment Simon's voice came bellowing furiously from the hall.

"Fenella! Fenella!"

"What is it?" Fenella called, opening the door and running to him.

"Get me a bandage and some iodine or something."

He held out his hand and she saw that it had a deep gash just by the wrist which was bleeding profusely.

"What have you done to yourself?" she asked.

Without waiting for an answer she ran upstairs to the nursery where she knew Nannie had everything for cuts and bruises in a medicine cupboard over the washstand.

It took her only a moment to collect iodine, scissors, bandages and lint. Simon was still waiting in the hall as she came downstairs.

"Better come into the cloakroom," she said. "I'll bathe it in case it's dirty."

"It's clean enough."

"How did you do it?"

"I didn't do it. It was that little she-devil Elaine. I managed to catch hold of her hand or she'd have stabbed me in the chest."

"Good heavens!" Fenella exclaimed. "What on earth's the matter with her? Why did she do that?"

"She's a bit angry with me," Simon answered and he smiled disarmingly. "She had a look at the picture and she didn't like it."

"Why, what's wrong with it?" Fenella asked sharply.

"There's nothing wrong, it's only that Elaine doesn't

51

like it. She wanted to cut it to shreds, but I stopped her and then she turned on me."

"Is the picture finished?"

"Practically. I've got another couple of hours' work on the dress, but that should suffice."

"Well, I'm not going to have that picture spoilt by anyone," Fenella said grimly. "It's my picture, Simon; you promised it to me, didn't you?"

"You're going to have a job to get it; Elaine will do her best to destroy it if she has to burn down the house."

"What have you done?" Fenella asked.

She had bandaged his wrist and collecting her things together she turned to leave the room.

"I'm going to have a look at it."

"Come along then."

She knew there was some joke that was amusing her Father. She hurried into the studio. There was no sign of Elaine and the picture was intact on the easel. She walked towards it, then stood still.

It was cruel, it was almost diabolical, and yet it was clever—amazingly clever as only Simon Prentis could be when it came to painting a portrait.

As she looked Fenella saw now that this must have been in Simon's mind the whole time, and she wondered, as she had wondered so often before, exactly what sort of a man her father was.

"What do you think of it?" Simon asked at her elbow.

Fenella drew a deep breath.

"It's brilliant, but oh, Simon!—how could you?"

"It just came to me in a flash," he replied.

Fenella realized that he was just as pleased and delighted with himself as any small boy who has managed to score off someone else.

This would certainly score off Elaine, Fenella thought, if that was what Simon wished to do. The picture showed her sitting looking into the three-sided mirror.

There was the beauty of her hair against her shoulders, the red gold of it somehow cunningly imitated by the frame of the glass, by the cupids holding up their scrolls above the centre mirror.

There was the softness of light flooding in from the background, touching the chair and table, reflected on the polish on the rounded legs and on the ancient carving. But one had eyes only for the face of the woman who stared into the glass.

She was beautiful, there was no doubt about that, but it was a faded, ravaged beauty.

It had taken Simon, with his amazing artistic sense, both to glorify Elaine's beauty and to destroy it.

He had made her far more attractive than she had ever been in her life; then he had damaged that attraction with a few strokes of his brush, and in the expression of her face was written very clearly fear and horror.

As one looked at the picture, one could feel almost physically all that Elaine was experiencing as she saw that her beauty had gone, that old age like some evil disease was encroaching upon the loveliness of her flesh.

There was something tired and middle-aged in the sagging forward movement of the coarsening body.

It was difficult to define in so many words exactly how Simon had captured and portrayed on canvas the whole tragedy of passing youth for a woman to whom it meant so much; yet he had managed to do just that.

One almost saw the wrinkles beginning to form round her eyes, the smudged chin line, the neck which had lost its rounded firmness.

It was a picture which would make many women shudder as they looked at it, but it was a picture which compelled and commanded attention.

For the first time since she had come to the house Fenella felt an impulse of real feeling for Elaine. She was sorry for her, desperately sorry. She knew what this must mean to her.

Not only would Elaine never again see herself in the glass without remembering this portrait, but her friends would remember it too; it was the type of thing one could never live down, that one would never be allowed to forget—Simon Prentis' portrait of dying youth.

No wonder Elaine had tried to destroy something that must have hurt her more than she had ever been hurt in her life before.

"Where is she?" Fenella asked her father.

"Upstairs, I suppose—packing."

Fenella looked at him.

"Don't you mind?" she asked quietly.

Simon shrugged his shoulders.

"Why should I?"

"She's fond of you I think."

"She's the sort who will only be fond of one person in her life," Simon answered, "and that's herself. I don't think you need trouble your head about her. The Elaines of this world will always fall on their feet."

"If she means so little to you," Fenella asked, "why . . ?"

She couldn't go on, somehow she could not put what she wished to say into words that could be decently spoken between father and daughter.

Simon hesitated for a moment, Fenella thought he was going to shout at her for daring to question him, and then surprisingly, in a voice that was unusually quiet, he answered her truthfully:

"I'm lonely, Fenella. Can't you understand that?"

"I think we all are," Fenella replied; "but you'll never be less lonely with someone like Elaine."

Simon sighed.

"I suppose you're right, but I go on hoping. I suppose I always shall until I'm too old."

He spoke the last words slowly and deliberately. Fenella looked at him and then on an impulse moved across to his side and slipped her arm through his.

"Why don't you come home a bit more?" she asked coaxingly. "When you get your leave, don't go up to London, it only makes you restless. We could ask people down here if you like, people who would interest and amuse you."

"And where are they—these charming, mythical friends?" Simon asked.

Suddenly he shook off her arm and walked across the room. He paced up and down for a moment, then raised his hands above his head.

"I'm sick of it," he shouted; "sick of it, I tell you—the whole damn, crazy boredom of it!"

"Of what?" Fenella asked, bewildered.

"Of living and dying," Simon replied. "What do we get out of it? What do we achieve? I ask myself that, I ask it again and again and there isn't any answer."

For a moment he looked a little crazed, then as if he fought back further expression of his discontent he flung himself down in the armchair in front of the fire, stretching out his legs.

"I'm fed up," he growled. "Fed up with everything."

He rubbed his eyes, pressing them with his paint-stained fingers.

"I've got a headache . . my eyes ache too."

"I'll make you some coffee," Fenella suggested; "but, Simon, if your eyes hurt, oughtn't you to see an oculist?"

"Good God, no!" Simon started up in his chair as though she had stung him. "I'm not as old as that yet. You'll be putting me into glasses, giving me an ear trumpet, and the next step is a bath chair. Get me some coffee and don't talk such nonsense, for heaven's sake!"

There was a note of real irritability in his voice and Fenella without further argument went towards the kitchen.

'What is the matter with him?' she wondered. 'He never used to be like this.'

CHAPTER THREE

A sharp, unexpected shower of rain splashed on to the parcels Fenella was carrying in her arms and soaked through her thin coat so that she could feel the dampness of it on her arms and back.

She was struggling along, half blinded and hating the thought of the long pull uphill which lay ahead of her, when a car drew up beside her.

She turned with a glad smile, guessing it was Rex, but to her surprise it was Sir Nicholas Coleby. Before he could speak to her he had to wind down the window and she had a moment in which to be conscious of her own astonishment that he should have stopped.

"Can I give you a lift?" he asked.

Fenella hesitated, then replied:

"Thank you very much—I am getting awfully wet."

He opened the door for her and she got in, putting her sodden parcels down on the floor; fish that was beginning to smell through its newspaper wrappings, tomatoes which were bulging out of their paper bag, and other miscellaneous groceries insecurely wrapped in bags and pieces of paper.

"I was stupid enough to forget a basket this morning," Fenella explained, "and my arm is nearly breaking."

"I'm glad to act as your carrier," Sir Nicholas replied.

Fenella smiled at him, not certain whether he was being funny or speaking seriously.

He started the car and they drove for some minutes in silence, and then Sir Nicholas said in his shy, hesitant manner:

"Your Father very kindly asked me to come in one evening. May I take advantage of that offer to-night? I want to see Major Ransome and it is so difficult to get hold of him at the camp."

"But of course," Fenella replied.

She had the feeling that he was making his desire to see Rex Ransome an excuse for his visit and searched her mind as to what could be the attraction.

'Surely he wouldn't dare to come in a friendly way?' she thought to herself. 'His Mother's influence would be too strong to permit that.'

"How is the picture getting on?" Sir Nicholas asked.

He was evidently anxious to be conversational, but Fenella felt as though every question he uttered was an effort and chid herself for not being more communicative.

The fact was she was both tired and worried for reasons it was impossible to explain to a stranger.

"The picture's finished," she answered; "in fact, I went down to the village in the taxi which took it to the station, otherwise I should have been on my bicycle."

She couldn't explain to Sir Nicholas all the circumstances that had preceded that journey to the station with Simon's finished effort.

Impossible to tell him that she had been awake half the night or that the picture had reposed during the hours of darkness in her and Moo's bedroom so that they felt they were guarding it with their lives and neither dared sleep lest disaster overtook it.

How dramatic and ridiculous it all seemed now in broad daylight, yet yesterday evening, when Simon had finally finished the portrait which he had decided to call

"To-morrow", Fenella had been sure that Elaine would stop at nothing to prevent that picture being shown to the public.

She could even sympathize with her; and yet while she felt that Simon had committed an unpardonable breach of good taste in painting the picture at all, she knew that for the sake of the children the picture must be sold.

It would be quite useless to ask Simon to alter it. Once he had conceived within himself an idea nothing would swerve him from his original purpose.

So far as he was concerned, the picture was finished and nothing would have made him change it; he would far rather clean the canvas, and then Fenella knew they might wait for months before he would paint anything else.

It was Fenella who had made the final decision as to what it was best to do. She rang up Mr. Boggis and tried without sounding too theatrical to make him understand the urgency of her request that he should fetch the picture right away.

Luckily, Boggis was used to dealing with artists and the vicissitudes of their temperament, and when he finally understood he promised to send two of his men down the very next day to remove the picture.

"If it was peace time, Miss Fenella," he said, "I would despatch a car right away; but that, as you know, is impossible. My men must come by train to Creepers and I presume they can hire a taxi to get them to Four Gables."

"You'll send them by the earliest possible train?" Fenella pleaded, and Mr. Boggis not only had promised he would do so, but had kept his promise.

It was not until Fenella saw the picture safely into the crate and placed securely in the taxi that she breathed a final sigh of relief.

Even then she was not totally reassured until she left it at the station, walking away up the village even as she heard the whistle of the London train coming round the curve. Then only had she permitted herself to relax and to think of Elaine.

Whether the latter had spoken to Simon during the night Fenella had no idea.

She had not appeared at dinner last evening and they had all felt a little strained and awkward, Rex sensing, even before he was told, that something was wrong and making no attempt to recapture the joviality of the night before.

Fenella herself had felt depressed and she guessed that her father was experiencing a similar emotion. It was left for Moo, being the youngest and the most impressionable, to find the whole situation rather exciting.

"Do you think she'll come creeping in on us when we're asleep?" she had asked Fenella when they had finally gone to bed, carrying the picture upstairs to place it against the wall facing their beds.

"I hope not," Fenella had replied.

She had looked across the room and felt that she hated Simon's portrait of Elaine almost as she hated the living woman.

It was a nasty picture, she thought, and painted with a violent bitterness which had never shown itself before in Simon's compositions.

It made one despondent, even afraid, to look at Elaine's face in the mirror. One could feel one's own muscles sagging apprehensively as though in sympathy with hers.

"I'd like to destroy it myself," Fenella said suddenly, aloud.

Moo looked at her in astonishment.

"I thought you didn't like her."

"I wasn't thinking of her personally at that moment," Fenella said.

"I think I know what you mean."

Moo sat on the edge of the bed, cupping her chin in her hands.

"You feel really that Daddy is insulting all women by what he has painted there. He hasn't allowed us to have any beauty inside.

"Of course we know it's Elaine and that makes us feel different, but I believe people as a whole do sort of identify themselves personally with a picture or an illustration if it's well done."

It was Fenella's turn to look surprised.

"That's awfully clever of you, Moo," she said. "What made you think that?"

Moo looked pleased as she always did when anyone paid her a compliment.

"I don't know. I've been trying to think things out a bit lately. Perhaps I'm growing up."

"I'm sure you are," Fenella agreed.

She sighed, for the thought brought to her mind that ever-recurrent anxiety about Moo's future.

It was all very well for Simon, she thought, to paint a cruel, almost bestial picture of Elaine and call it "To-morrow", but what about their to-morrows—her own and Moo's, Susan's and Timothy's?

There was a to-morrow for each of them and the frightening thing was that they must all rely on Simon for what the future would bring.

● ● ●

"Yes, the picture's finished," Fenella said to Sir Nicholas, and wondered if he had said anything in between her last sentence and this.

Her thoughts had been far away and if he had spoken she had not heard him.

"Has your Father ever painted you?" Sir Nicholas asked.

"Lots of times when I was a child," Fenella replied, "but not since. You'll see a sketch of me in the Tate Gallery if you go and look for it. It's rather an embarrassing one. I'm lying naked, waving my toes in the air."

"I hope you've been photographed since," Sir Nicholas said. "It would be very awkward if something important happened to you like coming into a fortune or getting married and that was the only available picture the Press could find to use."

Fenella laughed. She had not suspected him of a sense of humour.

"You frighten me. I shall certainly go and get myself photographed immediately."

They reached the drive which led up to Four Gables.

"Don't turn off if you are in a hurry," Fenella suggested. "I can easily walk this little way."

"I'll take you right to the door. Don't forget that I offered to deliver the groceries."

"Thank you," Fenella said, and then on an impulse added: "Would you like to come to dinner?"

As soon as she had uttered the invitation she regretted it. She saw the expression of Sir Nicholas' face and sensitively took it to mean that he thought she was being pushing.

"But of course you don't want . ." she started to say.

Then Sir Nicholas drew up at the front door and putting on the brake, turned to look at her.

"That's very kind of you, Miss Prentis," he said. "I shall be delighted to accept if you are quite certain you can manage it."

There was nothing left for Fenella to do except to tell him the time to come, then she thanked him for the lift and jumped out quickly.

"Please don't move; I can manage."

She opened the front door and carried in her things. As she turned to close it she realised that he was still looking after her, making no attempt to drive away.

For one moment she had the impression that he would have liked to be asked in, then she told herself she was being imaginative.

'He may be lonely,' she thought, 'but not as lonely as all that!'

She gave him a somewhat self-conscious little wave of the hand before she shut the door behind her.

It was strange, but all the time she was preparing luncheon she kept thinking of Sir Nicholas Coleby. There was something vaguely wistful about him, she thought, and yet apart from the wounds he had received in the war there was no reason to be sorry for him or for anyone in such a position.

"I've got quite enough to do being sorry for ourselves," Fenella decided, "I wish to goodness Elaine would go away and have done with it.

When luncheon was ready she went upstairs and hammered on Elaine's door. There was no answer. Fenella knocked again.

"It's Fenella," she called. "Luncheon is ready—are you coming down?"

The door was flung open suddenly and Elaine stood there, looking, Fenella saw with relief, more or less normal.

She was still angry, there was no mistaking that, her eyes glinted beneath their heavy lids and her lips pressed together gave her an almost Mongolian look. She swept past Fenella without a word and started to descend the stairs.

As she reached the hall she spoke for the first time, throwing the words over her shoulder disdainfully as someone might address an inferior.

"Where's Simon?"

"I haven't the slightest idea. We won't wait lunch for him; the children have to have their meals punctually."

Simon finally appeared. Elaine looked up swiftly at his entrance and as quickly looked away again but not before Fenella had seen her expression.

'She really loves him,' she thought.

"I've been for a walk," Simon announced.

He seemed to bring a fresh boisterous wind with him into the small dining-room. He strode across to the sideboard, and looked at the dishes reposing there.

"Let's go to London," Elaine said coaxingly.

"I don't think I can be bothered," Simon said slowly.

Fenella saw the blood rush to Elaine's face.

'What's going to happen now?' she thought.

But Elaine said nothing and her silence was even more ominous than if she had protested.

Thankful when luncheon was over, Fenella cleared away and washed up, then went upstairs to finish the housework which she had left undone when she had gone down to the village.

Afterwards she helped Nanny with the children.

She was crawling about on her hands and knees playing with them when the door opened. Fenella looked up and saw that it was Rex Ransome.

"Is anything the matter?" she asked, conscious that she was flushed and her hair was untidy.

"No," he answered, shaking his head. "I came back to fetch some papers that I left behind by mistake and I heard so much enjoyment going on in here that I wanted to join in. Shall I give you a ride?" he asked Timothy.

But the children were shy, edging away from him, their voices stilled for the moment.

"I was getting them ready to go out," Fenella said, scrambling to her feet, aware that Rex was looking at her in a strange manner.

"I feel very untidy," she added self-consciously.

"You're looking very beautiful," he said.

Suddenly she found herself blushing and turned away from him in confusion to pick up Susan's coat.

"What are you doing this afternoon?" he asked.

"There won't be much of the afternoon left by the time I've finished with the children and the housework."

"Would you like to come with me?"

"Where are you going?"

"I am going over to my home."

"Your home!" she echoed in surprise.

"It's only about thirty miles from here, and I have got some furniture and games there which will be very useful once we get that barn Sir Nicholas has given us fixed up as a canteen. I thought I'd go and fetch them this afternoon.

"I've got my own car, you know, so I'm allowed to take a civilian passenger."

Fenella hesitated and was lost. It would be a change to get away from the house for a little while, to forget Elaine and all the other worries.

63

"We won't be late, will we?"

"I promise you we won't," Rex answered, and she knew that he was pleading with her to go.

"Well, I think it would be rather nice," she said, and ran towards her own room for a hat and coat.

As they started, off down the drive a few moments later she gave a little laugh.

"I feel as if I'm playing truant."

"You're doing a good deed," Rex replied. "I didn't want to drive alone and, what's more, I wanted you to come for a very particular reason."

"What is it?"

"Because I wanted to talk to you. I don't seem to get the chance in your own home. Are you always so quiet?"

"I think we all have to be quiet when Simon's there," Fenella smiled. "He eclipses us all."

"Not you. I don't think you could be eclipsed by anyone. But I miss the sound of your voice. Do you know you have a particularly beautiful voice, Fenella?"

Fenella was afraid of the sudden shiver of pleasure that went through her at his words. For a moment she didn't reply and then almost childishly she chose another topic.

"I do like your car."

Rex laughed.

"What a baby you are!" he said gently. "Do you always funk your fences? You'll learn to go straight at them in a few years and find they're not so formidable as you fear."

"I don't know what you're talking about," Fenella said defiantly.

"We're talking about you."

"Not a very interesting subject, I'm afraid. You see, I haven't been anywhere or seen anything—just sat here looking after the house and the children—and I thought when I was eighteen I might be able to join the W.A.A.F., but it was impossible.

"Nannie's getting old and I couldn't leave her with the responsibility of both the babies and Moo."

"I think you're doing a very wonderful job of your own," Rex said.

"There's nothing very wonderful about it, but I suppose I'm lucky really—much luckier than some people."

"Are you happy?"

Fenella thought for a moment.

"I don't believe people ask themselves that question," she said, "unless something tremendous is happening in their lives. It is difficult to be either very happy or very unhappy when you are doing quite ordinary things."

"That's true enough. Perhaps one only asks it when one is loving or being loved."

His words seemed to tremble on the air between them. They were both silent, gazing steadily ahead of them, each vividly conscious of the other.

'I'm happy now!' Fenella thought suddenly.

She knew that it was true; her heart was singing, she felt as though her whole being had suddenly come to life.

●　●　●

The library was cool and dark and there was a fragrance of cedarwood, beeswax and lavender.

Fenella stood in the doorway while Rex groped his way across to the window. He unfastened the shutters and the sunshine came flooding in revealing walls covered with books, furniture shrouded in protective dust-sheets.

"There's something very sad about a room that isn't being lived in," Fenella said, looking round. "I want to imagine this room as it must have been—with flowers on the table and a big fire burning in the fire-place."

Rex smiled at her tenderly as if her imaginings touched him.

"This was always my favourite room in the house," he said, "and it always seems to me more intimately connected with my mother than the drawing-room. She, too, loved this room. She was a great reader and I think also it held for her almost sacred memories of my father."

He walked across the room to Fenella and taking her by the arm led her to the mantelpiece.

"Here's a portrait of my mother painted by Sargent."

He pointed, and she raised her eyes to where there hung above the mantelpiece the picture of a very beautiful woman.

Her son's resemblance to her was obvious at the very first glance and the portrait was a masterpiece in so far as it revealed so much of character and personality.

Fenella drew in her breath. She knew instinctively that she would have loved Rex's mother.

There was a compassion and sweetness in her face that Fenella had missed so much in her intercourse with the women who came to her home.

There was, too, a dignity and a hint of reserve which became her as well as the folds of the purple velvet dress she wore, against which her jewels shone and glittered.

"She's lovely," Fenella said, realizing that Rex was waiting from some comment from her. "I wish I had known her."

"I wish you had," Rex answered; then as Fenella turned her eyes from the portrait he took her hand in his. "I would like to open this house again."

Fenella looked at him, uncertain and troubled by the touch of his hand; then as her eyes met his her glance was held and something magnetic seemed to pass between them.

She knew herself to be trembling, yet could not turn away, but must stand there, aware of some rising emotion within herself which held her spellbound. Suddenly Rex's arms were round her.

"Fenella! Fenella!" he murmured. "This is too quick; but oh, my dear!—I can't help it, I love you so!"

She made one little movement as if she would escape, before her head fell against his shoulder and his mouth was on hers.

She was captured, held prisoner by the fierce possessiveness of his lips, by the excitement which shot through her, almost painful in its intensity.

She surrendered to him, returning his kiss and knowing herself caught in wonder beyond anything she had ever dreamed or imagined.

"Fenella! Oh, darling . . you are so lovely . . I hardly dared to hope . . ."

Rex's sentences were stammered and then he kissed her again and again, his lips roaming from her mouth to her eyes, from her eyes to the softness of her neck.

"Please, Rex . . please!"

Her hands went out protestingly against him, pushing him a little away from her, tremulous and unsteady, her breath coming in short gasps, her eyes pleading with him for mercy.

"Oh, my sweet, forgive me, but I had no idea that you cared a little bit too."

"Nor had I until this moment."

He adored the softness of her voice, the colour rising childishly in a warm wave from neck to forehead.

"Darling, I can't believe it's true."

He drew her across the room until they sat together in the wide window-seat, the sunshine haloing them in gold.

There he looked at her for a long moment, then taking both her hands in his turned them over so that he could kiss the palms, giving them each a long, lingering kiss as though he gave his very soul into her keeping.

"Tell me I'm not dreaming," he said at length.

"I'm quite certain I am," Fenella replied. "Oh, Rex, it can't be true; I've vowed so very many times that I would never fall in love. I've seen too much of it."

The touch of bitterness in her last words was almost startling in contrast with the tone which had preceded it. Rex's fingers closed over hers, hurting her with the strength of his grasp.

"Don't!" he said. "Don't let such thoughts hurt you. It is your life that we are concerned with, yours alone— yours, and perhaps mine."

"Why perhaps?" Fenella questioned, almost fearfully.

"My sweet, I was only being humble," Rex explained. "Nothing shall come between us, nothing shall hurt this love that is ours. If you love me, Fenella, and will trust me to look after you, you know that I would lay down my life rather than that you should be hurt by any act of mine."

Fenella looked at him with an expression in her face that was as confiding and trustful as a child's.

"And you're quite sure you love me?"

"I loved you from the first moment I saw you."

Something quivered between them, magical and breath-taking, then Fenella laughed and for the moment the spell which held them was broken.

"That's not true," she challenged. "When you first saw me you thought I was the maid."

"I apologize," Rex said, "I should have said that when I first met Miss Fenella Prentis I loved her."

"Oh, Rex, it's so absurd really. We've known each other such a short time."

"Time never has counted in love," Rex answered seriously, as if a million men had not voiced the same sentiment before him. "Love either happens or it doesn't; you can't force it, you can't create it; Heaven knows what it is in reality!"

"Isn't it just wanting to give oneself completely and absolutely to someone else?"

Rex caught her in his arms.

"Will you give yourself to me?"

"I am yours."

Their lips met and time for both of them stood still.

It was a long time later that they looked out on to the garden with dazzled eyes, conscious only of the warm nearness of each other and of that strange electricity which made them vibrate in perfect harmony.

"I want you to see the rest of the house," Rex announced at length, speaking resolutely, as if he dragged himself back to reality.

But for Fenella as they walked together up the stairs

and through the uninhabited rooms and corridors it was just a meaningless experience.

Rooms, pictures, furniture, and curios were all jumbled together in her mind, overshadowed and eclipsed by the nearness of the man who held her hand.

"As soon as the war is over we will be here together, you and I," Rex said.

He showed her the great tapestry-hung state bedroom where all the brides of the Ransome family had spent the first night of their honeymoon.

The room was lovely and it had, too, a grandeur which made Fenella gaze about her in awestruck silence; then unbidden the thought leapt to her mind—Rex had come here with Elaine.

Until that moment she had not remembered Elaine, she had forgotten her connection with the man she loved.

It was as Simon's woman that Elaine had come to Four Gables; it was difficult to connect her intimately with Rex, to recall how much they had once meant to each other.

But now such thoughts came flooding over Fenella, poisoning her with their insistence so that she felt as if Elaine was with them, standing beside them, mocking them with her flashing eyes and slow, insidious smile.

"I don't like this room," Fenella said suddenly. "Come away—I want to leave it."

Childishly she ran to the door and was halfway down the corridor before Rex caught up with her.

"Darling, what is it?" he asked.

Catching hold of her shoulders he turned her round to face him. He looked deep into her eyes, saw the tears springing there and understood.

"Oh, my sweet, forget it!" he said. "I made a mistake and God knows I've paid for it. I can't be punished further, that would be too cruel.

"You must be merciful, you must help me because, Fenella, you are for me the only real happiness I have known since I was a boy."

His voice broke slightly and instantly her arms were round his neck, the softness of her cheek against his.

"Oh, darling, I didn't mean to be stupid."

His arms tightened round her.

"I want you to understand that this is so different. Fenella, I love you."

They clung together for a moment without passion and then in silence they walked down the broad stairway together.

Rex collected the things he had come for, piling them into the back of the car. In the dimness of the half-shuttered hall he turned to Fenella.

"Kiss me once again," he commanded, "before we leave our home-to-be."

His voice seemed to echo round the high walls and suddenly Fenella shuddered, half afraid of the gloom and of the sudden impression she had of her own unimportance. She kissed him, but her lips were cold.

"You're tired," he said. "Come along, we'll go home as quickly as we can and you won't be too late for a cup of tea."

Fenella said nothing. She felt as if the gay rapture of the first moment when Rex kissed her had been lost. Then they had been transported into another world. Now they must return to the one they knew.

Rex left the keys with the lodge-keeper, who was also the caretaker of the house, and turned his car in the direction of home. They drove in silence; only once did he reach over and lay his hand over hers for an instant.

"Are you happy?" he asked, and was satisfied with her smile and her soft reply.

As they neared the village of Creepers, Rex pulled up in a deserted lane under the shade of a belt of trees, stopped the car and, turning, held out his arms to Fenella.

"I want to kiss you," he said.

He held her closely, possessively to him, kissing her now with a fierceness which seemed to demand rather than plead for her surrender.

"I love you, Fenella—you are mine," he cried, and

repeated: "You are mine," as if he defied the heavens themselves to take her from him.

Fenella stirred and touched his face with her fingers. "Please, Rex, please listen to me for one moment."

But he wouldn't release her, holding her captive, his lips very near hers so that she found it difficult to speak.

"What is it?"

"Let us keep this a secret," she begged. "No one must know—no one."

"I want to claim you, I want to be quite certain that I shan't lose you."

"You won't lose me," Fenella answered; "but I can't bear anyone else to know—for the time being."

They both knew that she left unspoken the explanation—"while Elaine is in the house."

"I would have liked to tell your father," Rex said doubtfully; but when Fenella gave a sudden cry he capitulated. "All right, darling, have it your own way, but, Fenella . . . "

"Yes."

"I want to marry you very quickly; I want to make you my wife. I want to be sure of you." She didn't answer and he went on: "I might be posted abroad and I want you to belong to me. I want a little real happiness before I go away. Do you understand?"

"Yes, Rex."

"And you will?"

Fenella hesitated. Something held her back from committing herself irrevocably; and then she looked up into his eyes, felt the tightening of his arms round her, knew that her heart was throbbing beneath his hand, and cried out impulsively:

"I will marry you, Rex, as soon as you like."

"Oh, my dear!"

They clung together and never, it seemed to Fenella, had she known anything so wonderful. She felt as if the last barriers of her defence had gone, the last doubts. What did Elaine matter, what did anything matter beside the fact of Rex's love for her and hers for him?

'I wish this moment could go on for ever,' she thought. 'I wish I could die and know nothing more, just keep this joy, this wonder, this beauty, as a part of myself for all eternity.'

A car approaching down the lane made them start apart. Rex drew out his cigarette case while Fenella patted her hair nervously.

The car passed them and they turned towards each other again, but once more the mundane affairs of everyday existence had encroached upon their privacy.

"We must go home," Fenella said. "I'm sure it's getting awfully late."

Rex lit his cigarette and started up the car.

"When does your Father's leave finish?"

"I'm not quite certain, but he's not got much longer, I know that."

"Well, then, after he's gone . ." Rex prompted.

"We will make plans," Fenella finished for him.

She put her hand of his knee.

"I am so happy," she said softly: "I wish I could share it with everyone in the world."

"I'm extremely thankful you can't," he replied.

They both laughed, not so much at what he had said as from the sheer exuberance of their happiness.

As they turned up the drive at Four Gables Fenella gave an exclamation.

"I'd quite forgotten! Sir Nicholas Coleby is coming to dinner to-night. He wants to see you."

"What a bore the boy is."

"I'm sorry for him."

"Good gracious! why should you be?" Rex asked, and then added: "Oh, you mean his wounds—I'd forgotten about those."

Fenella hadn't meant that at all, but somehow rather than bother to make explanations she left the matter alone. As they drew up at the front door Moo was waiting for them on the steps.

"Wherever have you been?" she cried. "I came home to a deserted house and wondered where everybody was."

"Rex took me over to see his home," Fenella explained.

She saw the surprise on Moo's face at the use of his Christian name.

"Where's Nannie and the children?" she asked quickly to cover her slip.

"Out for a walk, of course."

"And the rest?" Fenella couldn't bring herself to say Elaine's name.

"I suppose they've gone for a walk, too," Moo replied. "There's no sign of either of them in the studio, but I can't imagine Elaine on a country walk, can you?"

Fenella hurried towards the kitchen to get the tea. Moo followed her, chatting away, full of curiosity and interest as to Fenella's trip with Rex Ransome.

"What's his house like?" she asked.

"It's lovely."

"Why did he take you there so suddenly?" Moo questioned.

Fenella didn't reply, and Moo stopped suddenly in the middle of the kitchen, a cup and saucer in either hand.

"Fenella," she said accusingly, "I believe he's in love with you."

In spite of every effort of will Fenella felt the colour rising in her face.

"Why should you think that?" she asked evasively.

"He is!" Moo said. "Oh, Fenella—you might have told me!"

"You shouldn't jump to conclusions," Fenella said in a voice which tried to be severe, but Moo wasn't deceived.

"Fenella, Fenella, tell me!" she said excitedly. "He is, isn't he? I half guessed it when I saw you drive up together. You looked . ."

"Well, how did I look?" Fenella asked defiantly.

"You looked sort of dewy."

"What an awful description," Fenella laughed.

"Well, if you prefer it," Moo retorted, "you looked like two cats who had been at the cream."

"That's worse!" Fenella exclaimed. "You are a horrible little nosey-parker and I shan't tell you anything."

"Oh, please, Fenella, please tell me," Moo pleaded.

"There's nothing to tell," Fenella said. "You've guessed it already."

"That he's in love with you and you're in love with him!" Moo exclaimed. "Oh, Fenella, how exciting!"

Then suddenly she stopped dead, her expression changing, and in tones which would have been absurdly dramatic if they had not been a genuine expression of her feelings she cried:

"But, Fenella, you can't!"

"Can't what?" Fenella asked in a startled tone.

"Can't marry him."

"Why not?" Fenella asked the question sharply.

"I'd forgotten—I'd forgotten Elaine. Oh, Fenella, you can't!"

"I don't know what you're talking about," Fenella said.

But her hand trembled and she dropped the saucer she was holding on to the floor where it smashed into tiny pieces.

"There!—look what you've made me do," she added crossly.

Moo took no notice, she was staring at her elder sister as if she saw a ghost.

"Fenella, do see, do understand," she pleaded. "Elaine and Daddy—and then you and her husband—you just can't, it's too horrible!"

"Oh, do stop being so ridiculous," Fenella snapped. "Get me a pan and brush, there's a good girl. This is not a moment to discuss anything, least of all my private affairs."

Moo turned away in silence and then as she came back from the cupboard with the pan and brush in her hand Fenella felt a quick pang of compassion. The child's lips were pressed together, her large eyes were brimming with tears.

Fenella set down the pieces of broken china and put her arms round her sister.

"Don't look like that, Moo darling," she said. "Everything's all right, it is really; nothing's settled and nothing is likely to be."

Moo gave a quick sob of relief.

"I knew you couldn't do a thing like that," she said. "Not you!"

She kissed her sister's cheek and Fenella felt that she was trembling.

"Don't get so worked up, darling," she said.

She tried to sound soothing and realized that her own voice was agitated and disturbed. In her mind a question was asking itself over and over again.

'What am I to do now?'

Moo, reassured as easily as a child who had been frightened of the dark, was smiling again; she picked up the tea-tray ready to carry it into the studio, and as she turned towards the door she said in a half-shamefaced tone:

"Sorry to be such a fool, Fenella. I suppose I'm just a bit touchy where you're concerned. After all, I'm not surprised that every man who comes here is in love with you. The trouble is we don't get enough of them."

"You do talk a lot of rubbish," Fenella called after her.

But the moment she was alone the smile faded from her lips and she raised both hands to cover her eyes.

"What am I to do?" she whispered to herself.

This was a complication she had not foreseen—Moo so sensitive, so on edge where their father's amours were concerned.

Of course to Moo it would seem a betrayal if she, Fenella were connected in any way with the sordid episodes which besmirched their family life and which Moo took so much to heart.

Rex and Elaine—there the relationship stood, and it was impossible not to sympathize and, indeed, to identify oneself with Moo's point of view.

"Why did it have to be like this?" Fenella asked, and walked towards the window.

She stood staring with unseeing eyes on to the garden. She was recapturing that moment in the library when, drawn by the magnetism of a man's eyes, she had known that first wild, passionate moment.

"I love him!" she told herself. "I can't give him up—I can't!"

She gripped her fingers together and knew that already Rex's power over her was strong. She ached now for the touch of his lips and for the strength of his arms holding her, she longed to hear his voice, low and broken, calling her name.

She gave a little sigh and realized that the kettle was boiling over.

As she made the tea she found herself whispering his name aloud: "Rex! Rex!"

Only yesterday she had gone about the house, worried by other matters, hardly aware that something of tremendous importance was taking place within herself. For she knew now that her love had been growing all the time, even while she was unaware of it.

She might have guessed it when she had looked at the clock in the evening as it grew near the time for Rex Ransome's return from the camp. She might have guessed it in the quick leap of her heart when she heard his voice in the hall.

She might have guessed it when she had gone upstairs to take more trouble over her looks than she had ever done before.

"Oh, Rex!"

●　●　●

Fenella, watched Moo as she talked to Nicholas Coleby that evening.

She felt as if she were being torn between two emotions—her love for Rex, new and overwhelmingly strong, and her love for her younger sister which had deepened through the years until it was the predominating influence in both their lives.

She raised her chin and squared her shoulders as if she was facing the world defiantly, but her eyes strayed across the room again to Moo and almost despairingly she turned towards Rex.

76

"Talk to me."

He was laying back lazily in the big armchair, his long legs stretched out towards the fire.

"You talk to me," he countered. "Tell me what you've been thinking. I've been watching you and you've been looking very serious, almost austere. What's worrying you, Fenella?"

"Nothing," Fenella answered in a sudden panic. "Nothing I can tell you, at any rate."

Rex dropped his voice.

"Is there anything that we can't tell each other?"

Fenella twisted her handkerchief in her fingers.

"I suppose the answer ought to be no," she said, "but it isn't. There are still some things I can't share—not yet."

"Bless you for the last two words," he said gently. "I understand, but always remember, my darling, that I am here whenever you want me."

He spoke the last words in such a lover-like way that Fenella glanced up apprehensively. Elaine, fortunately, was not in the room, having gone upstairs after dinner.

Sir Nicholas and Moo were in the corner playing a game of Corinthian bagatelle which Rex had brought back that afternoon from his home and not yet taken down to the camp.

Simon was glancing through an accumulation of letters which had been waiting for his attention ever since he returned home.

No one had seen them, and Fenella stretched out her hand and laid it for a second on Rex's arm in a silent caress, then she got to her feet and moved in front of the fire.

This intimacy with Rex was too dangerous, she was afraid that it would betray them, and yet she found it hard to ignore him even for a moment when he was in the room with her.

She knelt down to put a log on the fire, then sat back on her heels, the dark velvet of her evening frock billowing out round her.

"That's how I'd like you to paint Fenella," Rex said suddenly to Simon.

Simon put down his letters and stared across at his daughter.

"Paint Fenella?" he asked. "Why should I? Have you forgotten that I only like to paint red-headed women?"

"I'm not likely to forget that," Rex said with a touch of irony in his voice; "but all the same I would like Fenella painted."

"Are you pleading with me or offering me a commission?" Simon asked with a smile.

Fenella turned to protest, but Rex had already given his answer.

"A commission, of course."

Simon looked at Rex as if he suspected something unusual was happening; then he threw back his head and laughed.

"I like the situation," he said. "I've just finished painting your wife and the picture has gone out to find the highest bidder—now you commission me to paint my own daughter. It's a queer world, my masters."

Fenella saw a faint flush stain Rex's face beneath his tan; then slowly and deliberately, bending forward to flick out his cigarette, he said:

"Of course, if you are too busy, there are other artists."

He got no further, for Fenella sprang to her feet.

"Let me make this quite clear," she said. "I'm not going to be painted. I haven't time, for one thing. You'll have to wait until after the war when we can get a servant of some sort to help in the house."

"Better have your photograph taken for the young man," Simon said. "It'll very likely please him just as well."

Simon was being rude but Rex ignored him.

"I'd like to have a portrait of you, Fenella."

"Well, you won't get one."

There was an almost hysterical note in Fenella's voice.

"I'm tired of pictures, whoever they are of and

whoever they are painted by. No one is going to do one of me. Is that clear?"

Without waiting for an answer she hurried out of the room and ran upstairs.

In her own bedroom she shut the door and stood still for a moment, both hands pressed against her burning cheeks, before she crossed the room to sit at her dressing-table.

'I'm a fool,' she thought, 'I'm behaving ridiculously. Everyone will guess that something's the matter if I'm not more careful.'

She heard a door close and knew that Elaine had come out of her room; then she heard footsteps going downstairs and realised that she, too, must return to the Studio.

It was no use being hysterical about things, and Fenella knew that she must keep control of the situation and try in some way which was not yet clear to find an escape from her own difficulties.

She powdered her nose and went slowly downstairs. When she reached the Studio she found that Elaine was sitting on the arm of Simon's chair, her arm round his neck.

She was talking in rather a strange voice and for a moment Fenella thought that she was drunk; then after one look at her dilated eyes she knew the truth. Elaine had been taking drugs of some sort.

Fenella was not likely to be mistaken, she had seen women under the influence of dope before and she had grown to know the symptoms—a white face, dark, dilated pupils of the eye, and a slight thickening of speech.

'How silly I was not to realize it sooner,' Fenella thought.

She remembered one or two occasions on which Elaine had seemed sulky or queer; she knew now that it had been a physical rather than a mental process which had made her like that.

But it seemed to Fenella no one else in the room had any idea that anything unusual was taking place.

79

After a moment or so Simon got bored with Elaine's encircling arm and rose abruptly from his chair so that she fumbled back into it, emitting a little scream of pretended fright, lying there sprawled in an abandonment which appeared to Fenella disgusting.

She was not alone in her opinion. She glanced up and saw Moo's face and knew that the child was wondering what Sir Nicholas thought of their Father's guest.

Impulsively, Fenella moved forward towards Elaine.

"Let me help you," she said, and pulled her out of the chair. Elaine's cold fingers clasped hers and Fenella felt a shudder of dislike. Elaine pulled up the shoulder straps of her dress and smoothed her hair to be certain that it was not out of place.

Then she walked across to Simon, pouting her thick lips in the peculiar mannerism which she always used when she particularly desired attention.

"Simon darling," she coaxed, "you are being unkind to me—in fact you've been very unkind for a long time now. Don't forget what you promised me this afternoon—that you'd alter the picture. What about doing it now?"

Fenella suddenly stood still. It seemed to her that her father sent her a quick glance of appeal.

"Alter the picture!" Simon echoed. "I'm sure I didn't say anything of the sort."

He was bluffing and those who were listening to him knew it.

"You know you promised me," Elaine said. "Darling Simon, I want you to do it now."

Simon looked at his eldest daughter and Fenella answered for him.

"I'm afraid it's too late to do anything of the sort," she said. "The picture has already left the house."

Elaine's voice rose in what was almost a scream.

"You mean it's gone to London—to the dealers?"

"It went early this morning," Fenella answered.

"But it wasn't dry . . you told . . you said . ."

She was spitting and spluttering in her rage, shaking

80

with a strange intensity which was almost frightening to behold.

"Now listen to me," Simon said. "Calm yourself down, woman. "I've finished that picture and I never alter any picture once it's finished.

"If I told you a lot of fairy stories it was to keep you quiet, and if you like I'll tell you a lot more now, but the fact remains that the picture is done and nothing you can say or do will alter it."

Elaine opened her mouth and Fenella expected her to scream. She held her breath, waiting for a second which did not come.

Instead, Elaine seemed to gather herself together as if with a mighty effort, then she looked at Simon with narrowed eyes and there was a bitter venom in her voice as she said:

"You'll be sorry for this."

She turned to face Fenella.

"And as for you, you . ."

What she was going to say was smothered before she uttered it. Rex moved with surprising swiftness across the intervening space between them to put a hand over Elaine's mouth and propel her forcibly from the room.

It was all done so quickly that no one moved or said anything. The door slammed behind them, there was the sound of Elaine's voice shrieking out something unintelligible, and then silence.

Fenella felt her own heart thumping; she saw Moo's face, white and distressed, Sir Nicholas' astonished countenance, and her Father's complete unconcern. He was not acting or pretending; such scenes never had the power to move him.

Now he gave a quiet chuckle to himself as if the whole episode amused him and taking a cigar from the case in his pocket he clipped the end with care and precision before putting it in his mouth.

"Fenella!"

There was appeal in Moo's voice.

"It's quite a warm evening," Fenella said in a voice that trembled although she tried to make it appear unconcerned. "Why don't we put on our coats and go for a little walk? I feel as if a breath of air would do us all good."

"Count me out," Simon said, sinking down in the armchair which Rex had recently vacated. "I've had one walk to-day and that was quite enough for me."

"What do you say, Moo?"

Fenella tried to smile at her sister.

"I think it would be nice," Moo answered.

Her voice shook and Fenella knew it was an effort for her to speak naturally.

"We've no reason to go upstairs," she said quickly. "There are some old coats in the cloakroom."

She opened the door into the hall apprehensively, but there was no sign either of Elaine or Rex. She had known that Rex would somehow get Elaine up to her room away from Moo and she blessed him for his quickness of action.

"We can't go on living like this," she told herself.

She felt Moo's hand slip into hers and gave it an answering pressure of reassurance.

They put on their coats, Sir Nicholas helping them, and walked out on to the drive.

As Fenella had said, it was a lovely night; the rain in the morning had given the earth a fresh fragrance which had been lacking during the days of continued sunshine prevailing for the last few weeks.

There was a young moon and the stars were glimmering over the high trees bordering the drive.

"I love this time of the evening," Sir Nicholas said suddenly.

"So do I," Fenella replied.

"When I left hospital," he went on, "I couldn't sleep, and I had the feeling, too, that I was being suffocated. I used to make my nurse darken the lamp, pull back the curtains and open the windows so that I could look out on to the night and think.

"I thought a lot of strange things during those hours when everyone else was asleep."

In the darkness his voice had lost its habitual shyness.

Fenella, walking beside him with Moo hanging on her arm, felt herself interested and a little intrigued by these unexpected revelations, despite the fact that she was preoccupied with her own troubles.

"What did you think about?" she asked.

"Of life and death fundamentally," Sir Nicholas replied. "I suppose being so near death does jolt one out of a rut. Up to then I had been content to take life as it came and to find the world a pretty jolly place on the whole. Then when I thought I was never going to be able to walk again, I had to readjust myself—it was not easy for many reasons."

There was a sudden reserve in his voice as he spoke the last few words and Fenella wondered if those 'many reasons' included his mother and the cast-iron traditions of his home.

"One forgets that other people have troubles too."

It was Moo who spoke, her voice very young and clear.

"I think we all have them," Sir Nicholas answered. "They may be of one kind and they may be of another, but everyone seems fated to be burdened with a host of difficulties which somehow or other they have to break through and overcome."

There was a moment's silence, then Fenella said:

"Don't think I'm being rude, but somehow I didn't expect you to talk like this."

"What did you expect of me?" Sir Nicholas asked. "A lot of youthful blatherings?"

"No, of course not," Fenella said insincerely.

"The whole trouble with most of us," he went on, "is that we get preconceived ideas about people."

"We can't help it, can we?" Moo said.

There was a suspicion of a sob in her voice.

"We ought to try to help it; but, after all, I don't think it matters very much because when you get to know people and to like them, nothing matters but one's own impressions."

'He's trying to tell us that he likes us,' Fenella thought.

Her heart warmed towards the young man who was revealing himself now when they could not see his face as he had never seemed able to do in the light.

"Will you forgive me if I say something?" Sir Nicholas asked.

"We can't forgive you until we know what it is," Fenella answered.

"Well, it's rather cheek on my part," he said, "but I think you've had a raw deal up here. I've heard things, of course I have, living in this neighbourhood, and Moo has told me, too, what she feels about the things that have been said.

"Well, it's a damned shame and I just wanted to say, if you want a friend at any time, won't you please think of me?"

He spoke so simply and so seriously that Fenella felt the tears start in her eyes.

It was her turn to be tongue-tied, to have difficulty in finding words in which to express herself; and then as she stammered a word of thanks, Moo left her side and moving round beside Nicholas slipped her arm through his.

"I think that's wonderful of you," Fenella heard her say. The thought came to her how simplified everything would be if only Moo were a few years older.

If Moo could have married someone like Sir Nicholas, there would have been no more need to worry about the child; but they would have to wait another three years at least before they could begin match-making on Moo's account.

"Thank you, Sir Nicholas," Fenella said again.

"I suppose I . ." He stopped.

"Yes?" Fenella prompted.

"I suppose I couldn't ask you to call me Nick? Nobody calls me Sir Nicholas except my solicitors and it makes me feel most frightfully old and pompous."

"But of course we'd love to," Fenella answered. "I

don't think we need tell you what our nicknames are, you've heard them often enough."

"I'd like you to call me Miranda," Moo said. "I think Moo is a ridiculous name and most undignified."

Fenella laughed.

"You can't be dignified yet, and Miranda sounds even more pompous than Sir Nicholas. You'll have to be Moo a little longer; then when you are grown up we will put it in the papers that Miss Moo Prentis wishes in future to be known as Miss Miranda and communications addressed in any other way will not be acknowledged."

They were laughing as Rex came up to them, moving down the drive, a dark shape unexpectedly tall when he was away from the shadow of the trees.

Fenella saw him first and felt her heart leap out as if to meet him, and then he was beside them, his arm through Fenella's, his hands seeking hers in the warm intimacy of her coat pocket.

"I think it was a mean trick of you all to run away like that," he said.

"We thought it was too lovely a night to miss," Fenella replied.

"How right you were," he answered. "There's nothing more perfect than an English evening with the moon just rising, the stars coming out and the good rich smell of the earth."

"I've often wondered what the earth did smell of exactly," Nicholas said.

There was a slight stammer in his voice again and Fenella knew that his confidence had passed now that Rex had joined them.

"There are no words to describe anything that really matters," Rex said sweepingly, "just the same as there are no words to express love or hatred, happiness or sorrow. One can only feel such things."

Fenella felt his fingers tighten round hers and then— she was not quite certain how it was arranged— Nicholas and Moo had wandered on ahead of them and a few moments later she and Rex were alone.

"Come here," he said, "I want you."

He drew her off the driveway on to the grass and then, shaded by a great oak tree, she was in his arms.

"This is mad," she protested. "The others will miss us."

"Does it matter?" he asked. "Does anything matter except this?"

He kissed her and she felt a flame run searingly through her. She trembled because she could not withstand him; she nestled close against him.

He swept her into his arms, holding her tighter and tighter until she felt as if all the breath in her body had gone, leaving her limp, almost faint with the intensity of her own emotions.

"Oh, my darling!" he said. "I've wanted you so. It seems a century since we were together, since I last kissed you, last felt you here close beside me. I want to touch you. I want to tell you that you belong to me."

In that moment of wonder and pulsating happiness there came to Fenella's mind the horrible nauseating thought that only a few minutes before he had been touching Elaine.

It had meant nothing to him, she knew that, and yet vividly she could see his hand, the hand that was now clasping her so lovingly, so possessively, tight across Elaine's open mouth; she could see him propelling her through the door, using force, almost brute force, against that thin, sinuous body.

'I won't think such things, I won't!' Fenella told herself.

Yet she couldn't escape them, they flooded in on her, evil skeleton fingers plucking away at her happiness until it was defenceless, quivering and unprotected.

"Rex, I'm frightened."

She whispered the words, but he heard them.

"I understand," he said, "but don't let anything frighten you. I'm going to take you away from all this. I'll see your father in the morning."

Fenella gave a cry of protest.

"No, I mean that," he said. "I've got to look after

you now, you've given me the right to do that, and we can't go on like this. This is no life for you and I'm not going to stand for it."

"Oh, give me time . . don't do anything yet . . you promised!"

"Your well-being is more important to me than any promise," Rex answered.

He held her yet more tightly against him. "You've never had anyone to look after you before. I'm going to do that now. You just leave everything to me, Fenella, and my sweet—I promise you that I will make you happy or die in the attempt."

He kissed her and she could no longer voice her protests. Her lips moved beneath his, but he silenced them.

'Why not let Rex do what he wants?' she thought. 'Why fight any longer?'

Life had got beyond her control. All she wanted was Rex' arms round her and the rapture of his lips on hers.

"I love you!"

She heard her own voice as though it was that of a stranger warm and shaken by a passion which she had not known before that she was capable of feeling.

CHAPTER FOUR

Fenella walked swiftly through the wood until she came to a small clearing where there was an old broken-down rustic seat.

It was half hidden by undergrowth and sheltered by the overhanging branches of two great chestnut trees. It had been a favourite place of escape for Fenella, Raymond and Moo ever since they had been babies.

If things went wrong they would hide there, to nurse their wounds in secret or to confide in each other and plot together so that they might combat a common enemy.

To-day Fenella was alone and yet the place held so many memories that she felt just being there comforted her and assuaged in some little way her tragic, overwhelming misery.

She sank down on the seat and covered her face with her hands. She did not cry, she felt indeed as if she was beyond tears, as if she was so near to despair as to feel herself already lost, utterly bereft, without even the strength to cry out for help.

The preceding night and day seemed to have robbed her of everything save life itself and that now moved sluggishly, with an inertia, through her veins.

'It can't be true,' she thought dully.

The things that had happened seemed in retrospect

like some evil, horrible dream from which she could not awake.

She was too miserable even to ask herself what she could do; she could only sit feeling dully grateful for the silence and the relief of being away from people, from voices and from Moo's persistent, almost unbearable tears.

Poor little Moo! Fenella could understand and sympathize with her even while her own position was too agonizing to be endured. Moo must be attended to first of all, the child was perilously near to hysteria.

All through the night Fenella had held her in her arms, kept awake by her frenzied misery which would break out afresh every time Fenella thought that she had dozed off into an uneasy sleep.

"I can't bear it, Fenella!" she had repeated over and over again. "I can't stand it. I won't go back to school, never, never—you promise me that."

"I promise you," Fenella said, repeating her words patiently and soothingly.

"But what will happen to me?"

"You shall go away to another school."

"But they won't take me; they'll hear about it there. I've got to give a name, haven't I?—and when they know who I am they'll refuse—you see if they won't."

"I'm sure they wouldn't be so unjust," Fenella argued.

"And supposing they did take me," Moo went on, "just imagine what would happen when the girls heard about it—all of them sniggering and giggling behind my back, whispering to each other. Fenella, I can't bear it, I can't!"

Fenella felt as if she couldn't bear it either and yet what could they do? They were caught as if in a tunnel from which it was impossible to escape.

They had to go forward, had to go on praying and hoping that they might see some light ahead, some relief from the utter darkness that surrounded them.

Even if Elaine lived things would not be much better. Fenella turned the problem over and over in her brain, wondering whether the slender chance of Elaine's survival was going to make it worse for them all than if she died outright.

Either way there was no escaping the scandal, the horror of police investigation, the misery of publicity.

She felt she would never forget that ghastly moment when Dr. Wood had told them that the police must be informed of what had occurred.

Until that moment they had been too agitated by events to think of anything save Elaine herself. It was then that Fenella knew it would have been wiser to have destroyed the letter Elaine had written, the letter telling them that she had taken an overdose of the drug she had in her possession and exactly why she had done so.

'If only I'd had the sense,' Fenella thought now, 'to have taken that note away from Simon and destroyed it.'

Yet with a sense of fatality she felt that such an action would have been certain to be found out sooner or later and would have implicated them in still further trouble.

But if Elaine's passionate reproaches to Simon had not been there in black and white, perhaps . .

Fenella pulled herself up with a jerk. What was the use of speculating?

The fact remained that at this moment Elaine lay perilously near death, and in the hands of the police was a letter in which she stated she was preparing to kill herself for love of Simon Prentis.

The horrifying, ghastly moment when they had discovered her lying on the floor of her bedroom was seared deeply into Fenella's mind so that she felt the picture of it would remain with her always.

It was Moo who had found her first—'It would be!' Fenella thought grimly—things happened like that in life.

Simon had said casually as he finished his breakfast:

"Run up and tell Elaine that I'm thinking of going to London on the afternoon train. She can come with me if she likes."

"You're going away to-day?" Fenella asked from the end of the table.

He had smiled at her and yet somehow she had fancied there was something shamefaced and a little apologetic in his voice as he said:

"I think it's time you saw the last of me, at any rate for a little while."

"You know I don't want you to go," Fenella said, "but . . ."

"Well, go on, say it," he commanded.

"Very well then," Fenella had replied. "I don't think scenes like the one which took place last night are good for Moo."

She had been half afraid at her own courage in saying such a thing. Simon was not an easy person to rebuke. He got up abruptly from the table and walked towards the window.

"I'm getting too old for them," he said, "but Moo's only a child."

"She's fifteen," Fenella had replied. "She feels things very deeply. Simon, do you think it would be possible . . ?"

The request died on her lips, for at that moment they heard Moo's voice screaming their names, shouting for help.

"Daddy! Fenella! Come quickly . . oh, come quickly!"

Fenella had run up the stairs, arriving there a few seconds before Simon. She had indeed touched Elaine and thought that she was dead before he reached the doorway.

Having written the letter in a moment of passionate anger and in a desperation which made her words fierce, resentful and bitter with suffering, Elaine had taken the drug and then, so it seemed to Fenella, had regretted her decision.

Even as unconsciousness threatened to encompass her she had struggled from her bed, had made an effort to reach the fire-place where there was a bell.

She was not to know, Fenella thought, that the bell was out of order, like most other bells in the house.

Elaine had fallen to the ground, her arm outstretched, her fingers curved a little so that they resembled a claw.

The expression on her face was horrible, the eyes wide open, the lips drawn back from her teeth; little wonder that Moo had clung to Fenella screaming.

They had sent for the doctor. It was perhaps part of the usual bad luck which dogged the Prentis family, Fenella thought, that old Doctor Henderson whom they had known since they had been children should have died nearly a year ago.

The new man, Dr. Wood, was young, competent, and inhuman. The villagers did not care for him, for a case was a case and nothing more so far as he was concerned. Old Dr. Henderson had said before he died:

"I've healed as many souls as bodies in my life and made a better job of many of them, too."

Dr. Wood was not concerned with souls and, what was more, Fenella felt from the moment he entered the house that he was prejudiced against Simon Prentis and his family.

His very way of speaking to them seemed to breathe antagonism and she would not have been surprised if he had openly accused them of murdering Elaine.

He certainly showed Simon in no uncertain fashion that he thought of him as accessory to the fact, and his manner was echoed by the competent, starchy nurse who arrived with the ambulance to take Elaine away.

Simon had neither been annoyed nor forced into a position of humility by this attitude; he had merely withdrawn into his studio and started to paint.

He could have done nothing more calculated to convince Dr. Wood that he was dealing with a man who was indeed a monster of depravity.

Anger he could perhaps have understood and made excuses for; shame was what he had expected; Simon's apparent indifference made him both irritated and vengeful.

Only Fenella understood her Father.

When Simon was upset he turned to the one medium in life in which he was the complete master; he painted

92

as a musician might soothe a troubled soul by playing the instrument he loved; he painted as a book-lover would seek forgetfulness and escape in reading.

People came in and out of the studio, spoke to him, asked his authority, questioned him, and still Simon went on painting.

He would stand back from the canvas considering his work from this angle and that, answer his inquisitor over his shoulder and continue to paint. He would not stop for meals.

Rex had finally taken charge of everything.

He had already left the house when Elaine was discovered, and it was not until the doctor started asking searching questions that Fenella remembered his relationship with Elaine and decided that it would be wise to send for him.

Dr. Wood had appeared surprised when Fenella had told him that she wished to send for Major Ransome.

Fenella knew how his mind was working and saw that for one second he thought that perhaps the whole situation was not as ugly as it seemed. The victim had a husband—that might whitewash her and make the whole affair more respectable.

But Fenella remembered that the facts of the divorce must come out; it would be known that Rex had billeted himself on Four Gables; it would doubtless be discovered that he had not intended to meet his former wife there.

She had felt helplessly as if she was watching an express train hurtling towards a crash yet unable to prevent it. And the crash would involve her life and Moo's, there was no doubt of that.

Fenella sighed a deep sigh which came from the very depths of her being and almost hurt her in its intensity. What a ghastly muddle the whole thing was!

"Oh God!" Fenella prayed. "Can't you help us out of this awful mess?"

It was a plea of utter helplessness, and then at last the slow tears came trickling down her cheeks, releasing in a flood that misery that she had kept cooped up inside her while she tried to soothe Moo.

At last she faced what she had been avoiding in her thoughts ever since yesterday morning. Rex—Rex and her love for him. That now was lost, killed more surely and completely than if Elaine had committed murder before attempting to die herself.

Fenella had seen the horror in Rex's eyes when she had told him what had happened and she had known, too, that that horror held despair.

She could hear her own voice, dull, toneless, monotonous. He had said nothing, he had not attempted to touch her, he had just pushed past her and gone into the house to see the doctor, to take charge of everything appertaining to Elaine's removal.

They had not had a moment alone all yesterday or during the evening; what was more, they neither of them sought it, avoiding each other as if by some tacit agreement.

Only now did Fenella acknowledge to herself that gnawing fear which had grown steadily into conviction that Rex was no longer hers and never could be.

"If we went away . ." she pleaded with herself, and knew that even then it would be impossible.

Alive or dead, Elaine must stand convicted before the world as her father's mistress.

Fenella raised her face from her hands and sat staring into the cool green depths of the trees.

Ahead of her she saw loneliness beyond anything she had ever contemplated before, a loneliness more poignant, more terrible, because she had once known love, once found in that springing rapturous moment of Rex's first kiss the fulfilment of all her dreams.

She shut her eyes, recapturing for one second the feeling of Rex's arms round her, his lips against hers. When she opened them again she heard a movement through the trees behind her.

For a moment she thought it must be Rex and despite her misery her heart leapt, and then she saw that the man approaching walked with a stick and realized it was Nicholas Coleby.

He came across to her and sat down beside her. She

looked at him without a word, and then he held out his hand and she put hers into it.

"I'm sorry, Fenella," he said gently, his stammer somewhat pronounced so that she knew he was agitated.

Fenella suddenly remembered her tear-stained face and pulling out her handkerchief wiped the tears from her cheeks.

"How did you find me?"

"Your Nannie told me you'd very likely be here."

"It was nice of you to come over," Fenella said dully; then added: "You've heard, of course."

Nick nodded.

"That was why I came."

"Well, you'd much better keep away. It won't do you any good to get mixed up with this; besides, your mother won't like it."

"I came to see if I could help you."

There was a note of rebuke in his voice and she felt she had been ungracious.

"No one can help us, thank you—no one."

There was silence for a long minute, then Nick said: "But I want to help, Fenella. Can't I?"

Fenella turned to look at him and saw that he was terribly in earnest.

'He's trying to be kind,' she thought. 'Pathetic, really. If we'd known him a little longer we might have been real friends, but now . .'

Metaphorically she shrugged her shoulders, then in a more gentle voice she said:

"It's nice of you, Nick; don't think I'm not grateful because I am, but what can anyone do?"

"It's damnable! It's you I'm thinking of."

"It's bad for all of us—Moo especially. She's sensitive anyway and this . ."

She made a little gesture with her hands.

"Can't you take her away? Can't you both go away?"

"I suppose we could, but we've got nowhere to go. Besides, don't you imagine that the story will follow us? It's bound to, you know, and Simon has a way of getting an abnormal amount of publicity whatever he does.

95

This particular episode isn't likely to be played down by the newspapers even in war-time."

"But surely something could be done?"

"But what?"

"That's exactly what Ransome said."

Fenella's fingers tightened in her lap.

"You've seen him, then?"

"Yes. It was he who told me, as a matter of fact. I'd heard some rumours from the village, of course, and so I went down to see him. I found him at the camp and he told me the whole sordid story. The only thing I wanted to do, Fenella, was to help you."

"That was nice of you, Nick, but there it is—we've just got to face it, I suppose, and hope for the best."

Nick cleared his throat.

"I did think of something, but you might think it terribly cheek of me suggesting it."

"I'd welcome any suggestion if it would help," Fenella said wearily. "It's rather like being in a nightmare, Nick. You know it's a dream and yet you can't wake up. I feel the whole thing's ridiculous, absurd, too frightening to be true, and yet I can't wake up."

She cupped her chin in her hands, looking ahead.

"It's Moo," she confided, "that worries me most. The babies are too young, bless them. Moo is absolutely frantic. I don't know what to do about her. She's asleep now or I wouldn't be here."

"You haven't listened to my suggestion yet."

"I'm sorry—tell me what it is."

She turned to look at him and to her surprise saw he was blushing.

"Why, Nick!" she exclaimed.

Then, hesitating, stammering so badly that it was with difficulty she understood him, Nick said:

"I wondered, Fenella, if it wouldn't help things a little bit if you married me?"

For one wild moment Fenella thought he was joking, before she too felt the blood coursing up her cheeks.

"But, Nick!" she exclaimed.

"You'll think it an impertinence, I know," Nick said

his words coming quickly as though they were forced between his lips, "but, Fenella, I'm certain that if I was your husband it would make things better.

"I might even be able to pull strings to keep the whole matter if not quiet at least quieter. You know what the people are like round here.

"I know the police very well indeed, I know the Coroner, too; he's a nice old chap who was extremely fond of my Father, but as things are now I haven't got any standing.

"If I go to see them they'll merely tell me politely but firmly not to interfere. Besides, you know what Mother's like—they'll listen to her rather than me when it's something which concerns the village."

"Yet you ask me . ." Fenella felt she couldn't say the words.

"To be my wife," Nick repeated firmly. "Yes, Fenella, I do ask that. I know that things would be different then."

"But, Nick," Fenella said, "I can't marry you like that, just to help myself or even ourselves—it wouldn't be fair to you. It is terribly sweet of you, of course and very unselfish, but you—you've got your life ahead of you.

"You've a position, a name—you can't spoil your chances, however generous the motive. If you tied yourself to a Prentis you'd regret it. Thank you, Nick, and it's very, very sweet of you. I shall always remember that I had one real friend who tried to help me."

Nicholas was gripping his stick and Fenella saw that his knuckles were white.

"There's something I haven't said," he remarked, "something I haven't told you."

"What's that?"

"That I love you," Nick said.

He turned to face her and his stick fell to the ground with a crash.

"I love you, Fenella, and that's the real reason why I want you to marry me."

● ● ●

"May I be the first to congratulate you, Lady Coleby?"

Fenella murmured her thanks automatically. She noted with some disinterested part of her brain that the Registrar's false teeth fitted badly and that his tone as well as his smile was mechanical and meaningless, doubtless from long practice.

It was a grey day outside with a promise of rain in the lowering clouds and the room was half in shadow—a fitting atmosphere, Fenella thought suddenly, for her own feelings of apprehension and dismay.

She heard the clink of money, saw Nicholas take up his stick and knew that the ordeal was over.

Their witnesses, an aged clerk in a threadbare suit and a frowsy-looking charwoman, offered their good wishes with the same mechanical glibness which had characterized the Registrar's speech. To them it was all in a day's work and again money changed hands.

Then Fenella and Nicholas were outside the door, both of them instinctively drawing a deep breath of relief.

The car was waiting for them. They got into it in silence, Fenella making no attempt to help Nicholas's difficult movements, feeling that he would prefer to manage things his own way.

He didn't start up the car immediately; he fumbled for his cigarette case, opened it and offered it to Fenella. She shook her head.

"I don't smoke, thanks."

"I ought to have known that, I suppose."

They looked at each other and then suddenly they began to laugh, and for a few seconds they went on laughing.

It was as if the sound broke down the barriers of restraint and cracked the dull misery which had gripped Fenella's heart for the last four days.

"I don't know why it's so funny," Fenella said at length.

"I think it was the Registrar," Nick suggested.

"His false teeth," Fenella agreed; "and those horribly effusive witnesses."

"I wish I hadn't had to bring you here," Nick said, speaking seriously.

"Oh, it doesn't matter," Fenella replied, "and after all, we've been lucky. There are no reporters."

"Heavens!—I'd forgotten all about them," Nick exclaimed. "Let's get out of here quickly. There may be one lurking around just in the hope of something sensational."

He started the car and drove through the winding streets of the little country town until they reached the outskirts, where he stopped outside an ancient wayside inn.

"Do you want anything?" Fenella asked in surprise.

"I want to drink the health of my wife," he answered.

At the unexpected word the blood came rushing into her cheeks.

She made no reply but got out of the car and preceded Nick indoors. It was a quaint old-fashioned place, oak-beamed with wide, open fire-places. There was no one in the sitting-room and Fenella sat down in a low chair while Nicholas went to find someone.

Alone, Fenella closed her eyes as if she would shut out not only the present but the future. She felt numbed, hardly aware of what was going on about her.

From that moment three days ago when Nicholas had asked her to marry him she had hardly had time for coherent thought or for reflection.

Events had moved so swiftly, for she had known even as she had instinctively cried out her refusal of his offer of marriage that it was inevitable for her to accept it; it was so obviously the best thing to do, the best thing for Moo, for the children, for them all.

It was escape—escape from the horror that surrounded Four Gables and the degradation of the situation into which Elaine had forced them.

Elaine was still alive, unconscious, desperately ill, but still alive. It was like hanging on the edge of a precipice,

Fenella thought, waiting for her to die and for the full scandal of her death to burst upon them.

But if she eventually got well the position would be no better, for then the police would start proceedings against her on a charge of attempted suicide. Either way it seemed to Fenella there was only one possible means of partial escape—to marry Nick.

As she had walked soberly and alone back to the house after they had talked together in the little wood, Fenella had known deep within her heart what her answer must be.

She had promised to give him her reply that evening; but before she reached home, before she told Moo what had happened and saw the quick hope and excitement spring into the child's eyes, she knew that in reality she had no choice.

And yet her blood cried out at the sacrifice. To marry Nicholas while she loved Rex with every fibre of her being was deliberately to destroy all that made life worth living.

She shrank within herself from the thought of Rex. She was afraid to voice even in secret her feelings where he was concerned.

But she knew in shame that she needed Nicholas because he threw her a lifeline. She must take him on what terms she could get even while she felt humiliated by the haste and desire for secrecy.

For Nicholas was prepared to be secretive too, as she learnt that evening.

"We'll get married first and talk afterwards," he said; and she understood all that he left unsaid.

She had met Nicholas outside the house. She had hated herself as she made some excuse after dinner to leave her Father and Rex alone while she put on a thick coat over her evening dress, slipped out of the back door and hurried towards the shrubbery where she knew Nicholas would be waiting for her.

He had arranged to leave his car at the bottom of the drive and walked up the narrow path winding between the rhododendron bushes to an old disused summerhouse built on the boundary where the estate of Four Gables joined the Coleby acres.

'I can't bear this much longer,' she thought a hundred times as the day passed slowly.

When she reached the shrubbery she said the words aloud to Nicholas.

"You're not going to," he replied. "I've already made enquiries about a special licence. We shall have to arrange our marriage very carefully to avoid publicity. I know you would like it to be as quiet as possible."

"But of course," Fenella said, and realized that she had accepted both to him and to herself the suggestion that they should be married.

As Nicholas had said, it required a lot of planning. But they were lucky, or else the very abundant tips that Nicholas handed round had the right effect.

At any rate, so far—so good, Fenella thought ten minutes after she had become Nicholas's wife, and wondered now for the first time what the future held for her.

She opened her eyes to see Nicholas come into the room followed by a voluble landlady carrying a tray and some glasses.

"What do you think I've found?" Nicholas asked, and he was smiling boyishly. "Champagne! They had one bottle left in the cellar. If it's corked I shall burst into tears."

"There'll be no need to do that, young man," the landlady said. "It's a good wine and you'll enjoy it. You two look as if you are celebrating something."

"We are," Nicholas informed her.

"I guessed it. Is it your engagement or your wedding?"

"You mustn't ask too many questions," Nick parried.

"Well, whichever it is—the best of luck to you. I've been married forty years myself and only regretted it a dozen times or so, and that's more than most people can say! And if you do quarrel—and what man doesn't who's worth his salt?—the making up is worth it."

She winked, rubbed the glasses with a corner of her apron, then opened the bottle.

"There—did you ever see a better cork?" she asked, putting it into Nick's hand.

She poured out the wine and left them alone.

Nicholas handed a glass to Fenella and raised his own. He hesitated before putting it to his lips and suddenly they were both very shy.

"What ought I to say?" he asked.

"I don't know," Fenella replied; "I've never been married before."

She spoke lightly, but poignantly the thought came to her that had she been with Rex she could not have said those words. But Rex would have known what to say and what to do.

Instead of this awkwardness she would have been feeling radiant, consumed by her own love, content beyond all contentment to be his, to know herself beloved.

"I must say something," Nicholas persisted. "Tradition demands it. Although words are pretty poor things on these occasions."

He raised his glass towards her.

"To Fenella—whom I love," he said, and his voice was deep if shy.

Fenella felt herself tremble and bravely she forced herself to look at him, to say in a voice which shook:

"I'd like to drink to your happiness, Nick."

"I am happy," he replied. "I want you to know that—I am happy beyond all words."

Fenella put down her glass.

"I wish, Nick, for your sake things were different, but I did explain and you said that you understood."

"I do understand—at least, I'll try to, but, Fenella— that doesn't stop my loving you."

'I oughtn't to have done this to him,' Fenella thought. 'It's wrong, criminal when he's so young.'

Yet she had been honest, she had told him that night in the shrubbery that she loved someone else. No names had been mentioned between them and yet she thought he must have known it was Rex.

She could hear her own voice, low and shaken, stumbling over her words, yet resolutely continuing as she stammered out her feelings.

"I love someone else—you must know that before we go any further . . I love him very deeply, more than I shall ever care for anyone again . . it's only fair to let you know."

Even as she had spoken she thought how crazy she was being, how irrevocably she was damaging her own interests and throwing away Moo's one chance of happiness.

Yet it seemed to her that the words were forced out of her by Nick's decency, by his kindliness, and above all by the love that he felt for her.

It was impossible to forget that he loved her; even while she was so concerned with her own difficulties, she heard it in the eager tones of his voice, felt it in the clasp of his hands; it seemed to tremble on the air between them—Nicholas's love for which she could only offer in return gratitude and pity.

When finally she had fallen silent she had waited apprehensively for him to speak.

'I've done it now,' she thought, 'he won't want me after this.'

Then Nicholas in a quiet voice had asked only one question.

"Can this man marry you?"

"No."

"Then we needn't worry about him. I want to look after you, Fenella, if you will let me."

'To look after her.'

Fenella wondered now if he realized how much he had taken on. It wasn't only herself—in fact, if he but knew it, it wasn't herself whom Nicholas had married— it was the Prentis family and the endless difficulties and tribulations which surrounded them.

That was what Nicholas had taken on and God help him! he didn't know how much it was going to ask of him.

Fenella looked up at him standing before her, the

103

glass of champagne in his hand, frowning with the intensity of his feelings.

Impulsively she put out her hand.

"Thank you, Nick."

He took her hand a little clumsily as if he were embarrassed by the gesture.

"What for?"

"For being so kind. I don't think I've ever met a man who was kind before."

He knitted his brows as if he found it hard to understand her, then abruptly he dropped her hand and crossed the hearth to sit down in the chair opposite.

"Let's make plans," he said. "Where do we go from here?"

"I hadn't thought."

Nicholas looked up at the clock over the mantelpiece.

"It's nearly eleven o'clock."

"Then it's far too early in the morning to be drinking champagne. I suppose I couldn't have a cup of tea or coffee?"

"What a fool I am!" Nick exclaimed. "I suppose you had no breakfast."

"I couldn't face it somehow," Fenella admitted.

"I'm hungry too, now I think about it. I felt rather a sinking feeling and thought it must be a drink I wanted, but it's really hunger."

He scrambled to his feet.

"I'll go and see what I can get."

"Would you like me to help?"

"No, leave it to me."

Twenty minutes later they were having breakfast—breakfast of coffee, toast and honey, with boiled eggs given them as a great concession, new laid from the landlady's hen-house in the back garden.

The bottle of champagne still three-quarters full stood forgotten on the sideboard.

"This seems more homely," Nick said, looking at the bottle and then back at the breakfast table.

"I've never enjoyed a meal more," Fenalle answered,

104

"and my chief delight is that I shan't have to wash up."

Nicholas passed his cup to be refilled.

"Fenella," he said, "have you thought of what we're going to do now?"

Fenella shook her head.

"I haven't thought of anything," she answered; then added honestly: "Well, I have wondered once or twice."

He took his cup and sat staring at it."

"I'm worried for you," he said. "I know that we've done the right thing in getting married as we have without fuss, without publicity, without out all the talk and palaver that goes on over weddings as a rule; but, Fenella—we've got to go back and face the music and it isn't going to be pleasant."

"I know that."

"My Mother," Nick went on, "is a wonderful woman, but she's difficult. She's not going to like this, Fenella, and yet I believe it's better to break it to her this way than if we'd told her before we were actually married."

"What shall we do if she refuses to see me?" Fenella asked nervously.

"She can't do that," Nick replied. "You see the house is mine, so is the money. I don't quite know why my Father made the will he did, but he left my Mother entirely dependent on me, a position I should, of course, never take advantage of.

"But the fact remains that in war-time it is going to be difficult to ask my Mother to live elsewhere. After the war it will, of course, be different."

"Oh, Nick, I wish now . ."

"No, you don't," he interrupted quickly. "You don't wish anything of the sort. It's going to be perfectly all right. I'm not going to have you worried, whatever happens."

"Thank you, Nick."

Fenella tried to smile, but it was not a very successful effort.

'He's frightened,' she thought.

Yet somehow she trusted Nick to fulfill the promises

he had made to her, promises which concerned Elaine, promises which would safeguard Moo until she, too, could marry someone to protect and look after her.

Fenella drew a deep breath.

"Hadn't we better be getting back?" she asked.

Nick nodded.

They got up from the table and Fenella moved across the room to where an old looking-glass hung over a chest. She looked at her reflection, tidied her hair, and turned round to face Nick. He was looking at her standing stiffly in the centre of the room.

"I'm ready now," she said.

He hesitated for a moment then he laid his hand on her arm.

"I want to kiss you, Fenella—do you mind?"

There was only a fraction of a second's pause before she answered:

"Of course not."

She raised her cheek towards him and he bent to touch it with his lips, then slowly he put his arms round her, drawing her close. Fenella was still, then suddenly as she felt his lips seeking hers she moved—a panic-striken movement—and was free.

She turned and walked towards the window.

"Fenella!"

There was a note of pleading in Nick's pronunciation of her name.

Fenella turned round.

"Nick, I've got to say this now. I told you when you wanted to marry me that I loved someone else. I thought you understood then what I was trying to say— that just at present I can't . . I can't be anything to you . . Nick, you must understand."

Nick moved towards her.

"I do understand, Fenella. I'm sorry if I've upset you. I love you and I suppose I'm a fool where women are concerned. I haven't had an awful lot of experience."

Fenella gave a little cry.

"Don't talk like that, Nick, it makes me seem so selfish, so horrible. It's just that I thought you didn't understand that I can't . . . well, I can't let you touch me . . yet."

"I understand."

"I oughtn't to have married you. It was an awful thing to do really, it was selfish and grasping of me, but Nick—you took me on those terms."

"I'm not saying I regret it, am I?" Nicholas asked.

"No, of course not, but just now I thought . ."

"Forget it. It was just a mistake, the sort of thing that happens after drinking champagne very early in the morning. Come along, Fenella."

Nick spoke abruptly. She realized that the conversation was over. Nick moved towards the door and she followed him, feeling an embarrassment and a dissatisfaction with herself which precluded all other emotion.

"Nick, you aren't cross?"

She felt lonely, as if he had deserted her, and she was relieved as he turned towards her smiling faintly.

"Why should I be?" he parried, and she had to be content with that answer.

As they came out of the inn a faint sun was shining through the rain clouds. Fenella lifted up her face and looked at the sky.

"It's clearing up," she said.

She wondered childishly within herself if it was an omen.

In the car as they drove off she found herself turning her wedding ring round and round on her finger. It was a very thin platinum band and she was glad that Nick had had the good taste to choose something so delicate.

They drove in silence until finally, as they neared Creepers, Nick, turning his head towards her, asked:

"You are all right?"

She knew he referred to her mental condition rather than any physical discomfort.

"Only apprehensive."

"You needn't be. I'll take the blows for you."

"I'm quite prepared to let you," she answered lightly. Yet as they drove up the drive of Four Gables she knew there was one blow which no one could protect her from, one thing she must face alone.

They drove round to the front of the house. Standing before the front door there was a car. Fenella's heart gave a horrified leap. This was something she had not anticipated—that Rex would be here now.

A feeling of horror came over her—so intense that it almost turned her faint, and then she saw that it was not Rex's car that was waiting there but another, an unknown vehicle. The relief was as sudden as the shock.

"I wonder who it is?" she said aloud, then thought: 'Perhaps the doctor. Perhaps Elaine is dead at last.'

She was conscious that her hands were very cold and that her head was throbbing.

The car came to a standstill. Fenella wondered if she had the strength to get out, then someone came through the doorway and stood on the steps.

It was a man. She looked at him for a moment unseeingly, and then she noticed his naval uniform and gave a little cry—a cry of utter relief and joy.

"Raymond!" she exclaimed, and scrambling out of the car started to run towards him.

● ● ●

Fenella told Raymond slowly what she had done and he was very cross and thought she had been a fool.

Raymond lit a cigarette, then sat down in the window-seat.

"Fenella, I'm not really being beastly," he said after a moment. "I'm damned worried about you, if you must know it."

"I'm beginning to worry a bit about myself," Fenella smiled tremulously.

"One thing is quite certain, whatever happens—this is the end of Four Gables."

"Do you think Simon will agree?"

"He's jolly well got to. I think I'd better go downstairs and see him right away and hear what he's got to say. I've only got forty-eight hours' leave and I shall have to hurry if I've got to listen to everybody."

Fenella looked at him and knew beneath his apparent

flippancy he was worried and desperately concerned with all that affected her. She got up suddenly and kissed him.

"It sounds ridiculous," she said, "but now you're here nothing seems to matter so much. I think you're right—we were suffering from inhibitions and complexes."

"Of course you were," Raymond answered. "The trouble is I ought to have told Father years ago that he couldn't bring his women down here. I suppose I funked it. He's not an easy person to talk to."

"Don't I know it!" Fenella exclaimed.

They both laughed, thinking of the innumerable times during their childhood when they had attempted to combat Simon and inevitably been defeated.

"Well, here's for it," Raymond sighed, getting to his feet. "You'd better come with me and clear the decks—I can't say what I've got to say with an audience."

"I shouldn't have a row with him," Fenella cautioned. "I expect if the truth were known he's awfully sorry inside for what has occurred."

"Just the moment to make plans for the future. And by the way, I hate to mention it, but where am I going to sleep to-night?"

"I don't know where I'm going to sleep myself yet," Fenella answered.

Suddenly they both laughed although Fenella's laughter held a note of tears in it.

It was so wonderful to have Raymond home again. She knew now how desperately she had missed him during the last three years of war. He had only been home twice—in 1939 and the spring of 1940 before he was sent to the Mediterranean.

Now he was back she felt that the burdens which had lain so heavily on her own shoulders these past months had been transferred to Raymond.

Even the unsatisfactory haste and secrecy of her marriage paled into insignificance beside the knowledge that Raymond was with her again.

Downstairs in the Studio they found Simon and Nicholas.

The former had stopped painting for the moment, but he still wore his paint-stained blue smock, and his palette and brush seemed only discarded momentarily in favour of a whiskey and soda.

Simon looked ill, Fenella thought, and for the first time she realized that her Father was getting old.

He could not withstand the strain of the last few days as he had been able to withstand difficulties, disturbances and emotional dramatics in the past. But it was difficult to pity Simon.

As Fenella and Raymond came in through the door he raised his glass.

"To the bride."

Fenella felt herself blushing as Nicholas turned towards her.

"What about a drink, Raymond old boy?" Simon asked; "and I hope now you will spare a little of your time for your poor old Father.

"You've been in the house nearly three hours and apart from saying 'How do you do?' you haven't condescended to have a word with me."

"That's just what I want to do now," Raymond said.

He looked meaningly at Fenella who, taking her cue, said:

"Come on, Nicholas, let's leave them to it."

They went out into the hall together. Nicholas shut the door behind him.

"You Father's been most awfully sporting about everything," he said. "I believe he's pleased."

"I'm sure he is," Fenella replied acidly. "People are always delighted to get their daughters off their hands."

Nick just looked at her.

"What's upset you?" he asked quietly.

"Nothing in particular," Fenella answered; "in fact, I'm not upset at all but thrilled to have Raymond home."

Nicholas said nothing, but Fenella felt he was thinking a good deal. She wondered if he was unduly perceptive where she was concerned or whether her feelings were unusually apparent.

"Let's go up and find the children," she suggested.

Then as she turned towards the stairs Moo came running through the hall from the kitchen.

"Oh, Fenella darling," she cried, flinging herself upon her sister and smothering her with kisses. "Nicholas told me. I was just looking to see if we had anything with which we could possibly make a cake. I'm so excited . . so thrilled!"

She kissed Fenella again and again.

"But I'll never forgive you both, never, for not taking me to the wedding. You might have let me come, Fenella."

"I'm glad you didn't," Fenella replied. "It was frightfully unromantic and the Registrar had false teeth."

"I should have found it romantic," Moo persisted.

"Oh no, you wouldn't," Fenella laughed. "You were expecting white satin, orange blossom, and bridesmaids carrying delphiniums. There was nothing like that about it, was there?"

She looked at Nicholas hoping that he'd understand that she was speaking casually and lightly so as to soothe the almost hysterical note in Moo's voice and calm the child's wild excitement and tension.

"It was a somewhat tattered setting for a momentous occasion," he said, dryly humorous.

"What's going to happen now?" Moo asked; "tell me."

"We don't know ourselves," Fenella replied.

"Oh dear, I'm sure you're keeping things 'rom me," Moo accused. "And fancy Raymond coming home so unexpectedly. I didn't recognize him when he came in, I didn't really. He's got so tall and so much older looking; but, Fenella darling, I'm so excited about you I can't think of anything else."

Moo paused for breath and then in a low voice, which told both listeners all too clearly how much the answer mattered to her, she asked:

"When are you going away from here?"

"We haven't thought or even discussed that as yet," Fenella said.

She looked at Nicholas warningly as Moo turned towards her new brother-in-law and clung to his arm.

"Nicholas, you will take me with you, won't you?— you won't leave me behind. Fenella promised, she did really, and you will keep that promise, won't you?"

Nicholas put his other hand on the child's shoulder.

"I promise you, Moo," he said quietly, "that whatever we do you shall be told and consulted."

"Oh, thank you!"

There was a sob of relief in Moo's voice and then she reached up and kissed Nicholas on the cheek.

"I'm glad you've married Fenella, I am really."

"So am I as it happens," Nicholas replied and Moo laughed.

"Of course you are. But I do wish you'd had a real wedding—it doesn't seem the same, somehow, being married like this, and Fenella's had that blue dress for simply years."

"She looks awfully pretty in it all the same."

Although he stammered it seemed to Fenella, as his eyes sought hers, that his words were bold.

She started up the stairs.

"Let's go and find Nannie. If we don't tell her soon she'll be offended and then we shall never hear the end of it."

Fenella left Nicholas with Nannie who was very pleased for them both and said she would show him the family album.

She ran down the stairs, heard the sound of voices coming from the Studio, wondered how Raymond and Simon were getting along but had no time to stop. She hurried into the kitchen and opened the door of the larder.

She heard a step coming along the passage from the back door and thought it must be George, Rex's batman, who usually delivered the groceries and things wanted from the village about this time.

It had become his customary and most welcome routine since Elaine had gone to hospital, for Fenella felt that she could not face the shops and the curious eyes of the villagers.

"Is that you, George?" she called out, then hearing the footsteps stop in the doorway turned round.

It was not George who was carrying the parcels and the carrier of vegetables, but Rex. Fenella stood very still for a moment; then white, but resolute, she moved forward to meet him.

"George had to do a job of work for a change," Rex said cheerily, "so I said that I'd be a messenger. I felt that the Government could spare the little drop of petrol I've used in such a good cause."

Fenella took the parcels from him.

"Thank you."

She put them on the table, striving to collect her thoughts, to find words in which to tell Rex what had happened since she last spoke to him.

While she hesitated he looked at her bent head and asked, his tone low and intimate:

"Fenella, what is going to happen about us?"

Fenella looked up swiftly, her eyes wide with pain.

"It's already happened."

"What has?"

"I've got something to tell you!" She drew a deep breath. "Rex, I was married this morning."

As if he needed confirmation of her words she held out her hand to him with its shining ring encircling the third finger.

Rex did not move, he stood looking at her hand.

"I married Nicholas Coleby."

Fenella felt as if forcing the words from between her lips was the greatest effort she had ever made in her life.

There was a long, ghastly silence, so long that Fenella was afraid and moved round the table.

"I thought it was the only thing to do," she said helplessly, her voice sounding weak and unconvincing even in her own ears.

"How could you!"

113

The words burst from Rex; deep and low as if they were spoken in the extremity of pain.

"Do understand," Fenella pleaded; "you've got to understand."

"And if I don't?"

He spoke the words harshly, then suddenly his hands went out towards her, taking her by the shoulders, drawing her nearer to him.

"I loved you," he said. "I loved you more than I believed it possible to love any woman—and now this has happened. It isn't your fault and it isn't mine, Fate has been too strong for us.

" 'The evil men do . .' Well, Fenella my dear, we can see and feel for ourselves the evil that women do."

"Don't, Rex, please don't!" Fenella was sobbing now.

His voice of utter despair seemed almost to break her heart.

"You might at least have talked it over with me," Rex said dully. "Surely there was some other method of escape rather than this?"

He released her shoulder and picked up her hand. He stood looking at her wedding ring, and Fenella remembered how he had kissed her hands in the library of his home, kissed them in a way which seemed as if in a simple gesture he gave himself into her keeping.

"Rex! Rex!" she whispered.

Instinctively she moved nearer to him; but he set her on one side firmly, inexorably, and moved towards the door.

"It's no use, Fenella," he said in a hard voice, "it's finished now."

She gave a little cry and covered her face with her hands.

She heard his steps, slow and heavy as though they were the steps of an old man, going down the passage; then the door slammed and she was alone.

CHAPTER FIVE

"My son tells me that you were married this morning. I cannot pretend that I am pleased at this news, but I shall do my best to accept the inevitable. You will understand it has been rather a shock to me."

Lady Coleby spoke levelly, with no other emotion in her voice save that of an icy coldness.

Fenella felt shabby and ill at ease and she knew that Raymond and Moo were affected similarly by the grandeur of her husband's home and by the proud, unbending air of its chatelaine.

Simon was the only one of the party completely at his ease.

He had exclaimed with delight as they approached the Court, commenting on its ancient architecture, on the swans moving slowly and gracefully on the silver surface of the moat which surrounded the house, on the heraldic stone newels which mounted guard on either side of the ancient drawbridge leading to the front door.

Fenella was conscious only of her own nervousness. She clung to Raymond's hand, aware even in her own distress of Moo silent and frightened beside her.

Raymond was not shy, but he was angry at the whole proceeding.

"The whole thing is ridiculous," he said to Fenella. "Any man who married you should take you home proudly with the flags flying. All this hole-in-the-corner business makes me sick!"

Fenella, however, felt it was inevitable. Nicholas had gone home after lunch to break the news to his mother and they had arranged to go over to Wetherby Court an hour or so later.

"I'm thankful you are here to support us, at any rate," Fenella said to Raymond.

She couldn't help glancing as she spoke to Simon who was at his most irritating, displaying an air of cheerful disinterest as if the emotions of lesser fry were no concern of his.

All the same, when they entered the house Fenella could not help being impressed by the size of it.

The wide oak-panelled corridors hung with oil paintings of bygone ancestors, the suits of armour lining the passage from the great banqueting hall to the drawing-rooms which overlooked the formally laid-out gardens, the cabinets filled with china, the heavy, carved mirrors and the soft-coloured tapestries which made Simon exclaim with delight.

Fenella had expected nothing so grand or overwhelming, and when she finally faced Lady Coleby she felt that she was indeed an interloper who had no right in a house of centuries-old tradition.

Nicholas was with his mother, and as he hurried forward to greet them as soon as they were announced she knew by the set of his chin and the expression in his eyes that he was both disturbed and unhappy.

He led Fenella forward, his arm through hers.

"This is my wife, Mother," he said.

Then Lady Coleby, disregarding Fenella's outstretched hand, had spoken her piece.

There was an awkward silence broken by Simon, who, quite oblivious of the fact that Nicholas was waiting to introduce him, was staring at a picture on the wall.

"Is that really a Van Fryson?" he asked.

"It is." It was Lady Coleby who replied to him.

"It's one of the most beautiful works of his I've ever

seen," Simon exclaimed. "Just look at the lace on that dress; could you imagine anything more exquisite? And the flesh colourings! It's a masterpiece. If only there was more of his work in existence."

"My husband bought that particular picture himself when we were in Holland."

"I'm sure he never regretted it, though it's a pity to hang it next to such trash."

Simon indicated the picture next to it with a wave of his hand.

Fenella drew a deep breath, she felt that this was not the right way to commence this auspicious meeting. She knew how difficult Simon could be when he got on the subject of Art. People were usually extremely annoyed at having their pet treasures described as "trash".

To her surprise, however, Lady Coleby smiled, a thin, wintry smile it was true, but nevertheless a curving of the lips.

"I am not surprised to hear you say that," she said. "I have never cared for that landscape myself, but this room has been left exactly as it was in my father-in-law's time.

"You will see that there is a mixture of Victorian furniture amongst the heirlooms. My husband liked it like that, keeping the room, as it were, a memorial to his father's memory, and I have always respected his wishes."

"You should never allow sentiment to interfere with good taste," Simon said severely.

He strolled across the room, inspecting another picture on the other side. Lady Coleby turned to Raymond.

"I think it would be best for us to get acquainted," she said, "before we start changing the house about, although doubtless Nicholas's wife will have ideas of her own."

There was no mistaking the touch of bitterness in her voice, but Raymond ignored it.

"You can hardly expect us not to have ideas as our Father's children," he said cheerily, "but for the mo-

ment we are all filled with admiration. You must remember we've never seen Wetherby Court before."

There was just a faint suspicion of reproof in his
voice and then he smiled and introduced Moo.

"This is my younger sister," he said. "Her name is
Miranda, but she is usually known as Moo."

"How do you do? I expect you'd all like tea. Will you
ring, Nicholas?"

Nicholas did as he was asked, and then there fell one
of those awkward silences which Lady Coleby made no
attempt to break. In fact, she allowed it to continue long
enough for them all to feel acutely uncomfortable and
then briskly she suggested:

"Won't you sit down? And do hand the cigarettes,
Nicholas, they are in that silver box over there."

Simon, however, continued to wander round, his
hands in his pockets, an intent, critical look on his face.

He was as unself-conscious as a child and it was impossible not to admire the sangfroid with which he managed in some peculiar way of his own to divorce himself
from the general embarrassment.

"Won't you come and sit down, Mr. Prentis?" Lady
Coleby suggested—like a general marshalling his
troops, Fenella thought.

Then to Fenella's relief the door opened and tea was
brought in.

The butler, old and almost decrepit with years, carried a huge tray laden with crested silver while a
parlour-maid nearly as old as himself moved a polished
table into position and covered it with a heavily embroi-
dered cloth.

"Only a very simple tea nowadays, I'm afraid," Lady
Coleby said. "Of course we are lucky in having our own
home farm, otherwise I don't know how we should survive."

Fenella, looking at the well-buttered scones, the
wafer-thin pieces of bread and butter, the sandwiches
cut mathematically to a pattern, wondered what Nicholas must have thought of the rough and ready meals he
had eaten at Four Gables.

'I'm crazy to have married him!' she thought to herself, and felt a kind of hysteria rising within her.

She wanted both to laugh and to cry—to laugh at the incongruity of them all sitting in this grandeur being patronized by Lady Coleby, to cry at the misery of the events which had driven them to it and her own stupidity in being stampeded.

"Sugar?"

She heard the question and looked up to see Nicholas handing her a cup of tea.

Their eyes met and she felt a sudden warmth within herself. Nicholas was sharing her own feelings, she was certain of that; he too was finding this moment unbearable.

"Another cup of tea, Fenella?" Lady Coleby asked. "No? Well then, suppose we discuss your future plans—yours and Nicholas's of course. I suppose you've made some?"

She looked from her son to Fenella and seeing the answer on their faces said briskly:

"No plans? Very well, I must help you. I'm afraid you've both been very impulsive, but still it's no use regretting it. It's done now and we must make the best of it—all of us. Don't you agree with me, Group Captain?"

"I'm sorry," Simon replied, "but I wasn't listening."

He smiled at Lady Coleby as he spoke and to Fenella's surprise she responded.

"Never mind," she said, "you can leave these little matters to me."

"I want Moo and the two younger children—Susan and Timothy, to come here at once with their Nannie," Nicholas said.

"I believe you did mention that you'd asked them," Lady Coleby said. "Well, I suppose we can arrange it. I understand that you intend shutting up Four Gables."

She addressed herself to Simon.

"I've no intention of doing anything of the sort," he replied. "Whose idea is this?"

Fenella felt herself quiver as she always did when Simon got annoyed. But Raymond was quite equal to the occasion.

"Your leave ends to-morrow, Father," he said, "and so does mine. We can't leave Nannie and the children alone at Four Gables if Fenella isn't there to help. Nicholas has offered to have them here for the time being and quite frankly I think it is the only possible arrangement."

Simon wavered for a moment and then he burst into a roar of laughter.

"By Jove, Nicholas, you've taken something on!" he said. "I thought you'd married Fenella, but apparently you've espoused the entire family. Well, you can have the lot with my blessing, but don't blame me if they prove a bit indigestible."

It seemed to Fenella from then on that everything had a kind of Alice-in-Wonderland quality.

Lady Coleby's dictatorial bearing, the house with its vast, over-ornamented rooms, Nicholas's embarrassment and ill-concealed defiance, Simon's assumption that he had managed to bring off something rather clever—all merged together in her mind until it was with a feeling of almost unutterable relief that she found herself driving home alone with her family.

They had decided on the double journey because, as Raymond had said, they couldn't arrive with their luggage before they had even said "How do you do?"

"We will see you about an hour before dinner," Lady Coleby had said graciously to Fenella. "In the meantime I will have the rooms prepared."

She made it quite clear, Fenella thought, who was to be the hostess at Wetherby Court and she could not help secretly sympathizing with Moo who, as they drove through the lodge gates, cried out:

"I don't want to go back. Let's stay at home; oh please, let's stay at home."

"It's too late to back out now," Raymond replied.

He slipped his arm through Fenella's as if he knew what she was feeling.

"Don't want to go back!" Simon roared. "You must

120

be crazy! The place is nothing more nor less than a treasure house. Fenella, I congratulate you—you've been more astute than I gave you credit for."

"Don't, Daddy," Fenella pleaded.

"And he's not a bad young chap," Simon went on. "Wants waking up, of course. I expect, if you ask me, the blue blood is congealing a bit in his veins, but then you can't have everything."

"I don't want everything," Fenella retorted unwisely.

"What's the matter now?" Simon enquired. "Damn it all, you've married the fellow—we haven't."

"I don't want to go there to-night," Moo said. "She hates us, you know she does."

"Nonsense!" Fenella answered. "Nicholas's mother is naturally upset, it has been a surprise for her; but Moo, you've said over and over again that you didn't want to stay at Four Gables."

"I don't know—I don't know what I want," Moo answered half in tears.

"We won't go back to-night," Fenella said suddenly. "I'll ring up Nicholas and explain. We'll go over to-morrow when Raymond and Daddy have gone. We'll have one more night all together."

"Yes, do let's," Moo agreed eagerly.

"It's your wedding-day, Fenella," Raymond said gently.

"I don't care," Fenella said recklessly. "We will stay at Four Gables to-night and go to Wetherby Court to-morrow. After all, when I got married this morning I didn't know you were coming home on leave. Besides, if we go away, who is going to look after you and Daddy? Somebody will have to get your breakfast, we hadn't thought of that."

"That's right, forget me," Simon said. "I'm only the breadwinner—the poor fool who pays."

He spoke facetiously, but Fenella fancied there was a hurt note in his voice.

"We will stay," she decided firmly.

She went towards the telephone, but as she reached it she felt Raymond's hand on her arm.

"Fenella," he said quietly so that the others could not overhear, "it's your life you are playing about with. I know what I should think of a woman who treated me like that the night I married her."

"It's different for Nicholas and me," Fenella retorted. "He knows I'm not in love with him."

"That still doesn't excuse your making him look a fool," Raymond said.

"Am I doing that?"

"You most certainly are. If you stay here you must ask him to come over too, otherwise you must go to him."

Fenella stood still.

"We can't ask him," she said, "there isn't room."

Raymond thought for a moment.

"Moo could sleep in the day-nursery for once."

Fenella turned her head away. She knew that Raymond was inferring that Nicholas should share a room with her.

"It isn't practicable," she said, and Raymond sighed.

"All right, have it your own way," he said; "but if it was me I should never forgive you."

Fenella took up the telephone. It was some minutes before she could get through to Nicholas.

"It's Fenella speaking," she said. "I don't think it is going to be possible to bring the children over to-night. They're ready to go to bed now and we're not packed or anything."

"Won't to-morrow do?" Nicholas asked.

"That's exactly what I thought," Fenella said. "After all, Daddy and Raymond are here until to-morrow morning."

"That's all right then," Nicholas replied. "I'll come over and fetch you in about an hour."

"But I . ." Fenella never finished her sentence— Nicholas had put down the receiver.

For a moment she stood debating with herself whether she would telephone him again; then she knew that she hadn't the courage.

'I'm a coward,' she thought angrily, yet felt it was all too complicated and difficult.

Raymond was coming downstairs as she went up to pack.

"Well, have you settled it?" he asked.

"Nicholas is coming over to fetch me," she replied, not meeting his eyes.

"Good," he chuckled. "Good for him, I mean. He's got more guts than I thought."

The telephone rang sharply and Raymond went to answer it. Fenella waited at the top of the stairs wondering if it was for her. It was the doctor and as she heard Raymond talking to him she came hurrying down again.

Elaine had been out of their thoughts for some hours—none of them had mentioned her even among themselves. If she was dead . .

"She's just the same."

Raymond put down the receiver.

"Conscious?"

"No, still unconscious but still alive. Actually, it's the best state for her to be in, you realize that."

"But it can't last for ever."

"Sufficient unto the day, my dear."

Fenella stood thinking. Raymond lit a cigarette. As he flicked the match into the empty fire-place he said:

"I've been thinking, Fenella, of what you must do."

"Now—this moment?" Fenella asked.

"No, no," he said impatiently, "in the future. I suppose you realize that as Nicholas's wife you are no longer exempt from war work?"

"I hadn't thought of it," Fenella exclaimed.

"Well, I should," Raymond replied; "and what's more, you won't like my saying this, but I think it's a good thing."

"What is?"

"That you should work. You've got into a groove, and the sooner you get out of it the better. I don't blame you, but if you ask me, the groove's pretty deep and if you don't scramble out of your own accord we shall have to drag you out."

"I think you're beastly."

Fenella faced him defiantly just as she had when they were children.

"People never do like the truth, but you've got to face it sooner or later however unpalatable it may be.

"And what do you suggest I do?" Fenella asked, half mockingly. "Become a Wren?"

"It's an idea, certainly, but I think you ought to consult your husband first. All the same, I should make up your mind once for all that even if you can wangle it your job is not to sit knitting socks under the direction of your mother-in-law."

"That's the last thing I want," Fenella said fervently. "Raymond, I think she's terrifying."

"Maybe, but I admire her all the same. I bet you she's always got what she wanted in her life and you'll have to be pretty nippy if she isn't going to get it this time."

"Why, what do you think she wants?"

"I haven't been taken into the good lady's confidence," Raymond said, "but at a fairly conservative guess I should imagine it's to get rid of you."

● ● ●

There was a knock on the door.

"May I come in?"

It was Nicholas's voice asking the question. Fenella sat up in bed, pulling her dressing-jacket closer round her, nervous and suddenly palpitatingly shy.

It was with an effort that she made herself answer: "Yes, come in."

Nicholas opened the door. He was dressed in the rather untidy, well-worn flannel trousers and the tweed jacket which seemed a habitual part of him.

She noticed that he was without his stick and that as he entered the room he supported himself against the door.

"Did you have a good night? I thought you deserved breakfast in bed this morning."

He glanced at the breakfast tray beside her, then added:

"But you haven't eaten much."

"I wasn't hungry," Fenella said, self-consciously.

She was aware that her eyes were swollen from the tears she had shed before she fell asleep. She felt very small and at a disadvantage, speaking to him from the depths of the big double bed with its peach-coloured hangings.

The night before, when she had entered the room which Lady Coleby had told her was to be hers, she had felt overawed by the vastness and grandeur of it.

Now, in the daylight, with the curtains drawn back from the windows through which the sun was streaming, she felt like a schoolgirl playing at being grown-up.

This couldn't be her, Fenella Prentis, whom no one had thought of any importance, now being waited on by soft-footed servants who addressed her as "m'lady", who had her breakfast brought to her bedside, who received a considerate husband at ten o'clock in the morning.

It was hard not to feel guiltily that she should have been down hours ago getting the breakfast in the kitchen; it was hard not to be frightened of everything and everybody.

Yet when she looked at Nicholas she realized that she need not be afraid of him. She had an idea he was nearly as shy as she was and she managed to smile at him as she supplemented her previous reply:

"I'm not very hungry, but I'm feeling very spoilt at having breakfast in bed. It was kind of you to think of it."

"My Mother always breakfasts upstairs," he replied; "and, quite frankly, I was a bit anxious about your seeing me so early in the morning. I have a feeling I'm at my worst at breakfast time."

Fenella realized that he was talking at random, giving them both time to become more natural, more at their ease with each other. Her gratitude for his consideration swept aside all other feelings.

"I'll get up now," she said. "I wonder if you'd take me home?"

"I've just been talking to your brother," Nicholas answered. "That's really what I came to tell you. He's got to catch the twelve o'clock train, but he'd like to see you before he goes."

"We'll see him off," Fenella said, "and then we can bring back the children and Moo with us—that is, if your mother is ready for them then."

"Everything's prepared, I believe. I'll go and bring the car round, so don't be long."

"I won't."

He turned towards the door, then hesitated a moment looking at her.

"You didn't answer my first question."

"What was that?"

"Whether you had slept well?"

"Have I got to answer that?"

"Any reason why you shouldn't?"

"Only that I hate seeming ungracious when you've been so kind to me—but I didn't, as it happened."

"I thought not. I was awake myself for some time. I nearly suggested coming in to talk to you and then I thought you might be frightened."

Fenella felt herself flushing.

"I was in a silly mood last night. I'm glad you didn't."

"We all get them at times. The next one you have, you might remember that I'm there if wanted."

"I shall."

Fenella's words were almost inaudible, but Nicholas heard them. He smiled at her, then the door closed behind him.

She jumped out of bed and walked across the thick-carpeted floor to the dressing-table.

'I look a freak!' she told her reflection in the glass.

Then she was annoyed that Nicholas should have seen her like that—and was then surprised at her own annoyance.

126

'He'd better get used to seeing me as I am,' she told herself severely.

As she splashed in the big, luxurious bathroom which led out of her bedroom she thought how many girls would envy her.

Most young women in penniless circumstances and with doubtful antecedents would feel it the perfect ending to a Cinderella story if they could become Lady Coleby of Wetherby Court.

Fenella told herself that and at the same time knew that her own reaction was not one of elation, and yet critically she was not particularly pleased with her behaviour up to date.

Her tears last night, for instance—she was ashamed now for having given way to them, for letting herself lie shaken by a tempest of emotion, sobbing as if her heart would break, yet able to control herself in so far that she could muffle the sounds lest Nicholas should hear them next door.

She had felt then that the evening had tried her too far.

The drive from her home to Wetherby Court had been fraught with embarrassment, for when Nicholas had arrived to fetch her from Four Gables she had begged him to let her stay there the night and received a blank refusal.

"I thought you were marrying me to avoid gossip," he said to her firmly. "If we part the very first night we are married that is one sure way to encourage talk and speculation."

"There's only your mother," Fenella protested weakly, knowing that she was fighting a losing battle.

"On the contrary," Nicholas had said coldly, "the announcement will be in the *Times* to-morrow morning. I have already informed the staff at home and by this time, if I know anything of Creepers, the glad tidings will be all over the village."

"Oh, Nicholas!" Fenella had exclaimed, her hand moving nervously at her throat.

"I want to make one thing quite clear," Nicholas said, "to all whom it may concern. I'm proud of my wife and I, personally, have nothing to hide."

He was right, Fenella knew that, even while she half resented his assumption of authority; everything, indeed, had been taken out of her hands.

Nicholas had talked to Moo and arranged for her to stay and look after Raymond and her Father; he had told Nannie that he would pick up her and the children next day, and almost before Fenella knew where she was she was in the car alone with her husband travelling towards her future home.

The evening that lay ahead of them was not an easy one. Lady Coleby was gracious with the unself-conscious patronage of a lady bountiful who has always condescended.

The servants had come forward one by one to offer their best wishes and incidentally to inform Fenella indirectly, but very obviously, that they considered her very lucky indeed to have married their 'Master Nicholas'.

By the time the hour to go to bed was reached Fenella was suffering from a sense of inferiority.

The contrast between Four Gables and Wetherby Court was in itself rather alarming and although Nicholas's mother was very much in possession Fenella could not help looking at the place from the point of view that one day she would have to manage.

The cares of housekeeping had been on her shoulders too long for her not to think of her new home from both the financial and the domestic angle and she felt herself appalled at the task which must eventually be hers.

What was more, she could not escape from the feeling that all this was a dream. It was so ridiculous to think that only a week or so ago she had not known Nicholas and yet here she was married to him.

More than once during the evening she had touched her wedding ring to be sure it was there, to be certain that she had not imagined everything which had taken place since eight o'clock that morning.

"I don't know about you young people," Lady Coleby said after dinner, "but I'm ready for bed. I'm afraid I'm getting old. I find such shocks as you have sprung upon me to-day, Nicholas, very tiring."

"I'm sorry, Mother—it won't happen again."

There was a touch of humour in his answer which Lady Coleby entirely missed.

"I should hope not," she said. "Once is quite enough for me, I assure you. I haven't reproached you, but it was rather inconsiderate."

"I know, Mother, and I'm sorry. My only excuse is that the circumstances warranted it."

"Well, it's done now," Lady Coleby gave a quick sigh. "I pride myself that I am one of those women who don't nag, but you are lucky, my dear boy. I might have been a very different sort of mother."

Lady Coleby's tone told them that they should congratulate themselves very heartily indeed.

Fenella wished that she could say something as grateful and gracious as her mother-in-law obviously expected, but found herself standing tongue-tied, feeling merely gauche and extremely self-conscious.

All three went up the broad staircase together.

"I hope you will be comfortable," Lady Coleby said to Fenella, at the door of her bedroom. "This was always one of my favourite rooms in the house. If there is anything you want you will, of course ring."

Nicholas followed Fenella into her bedroom. He shut the door and for a moment they stood looking at each other, before he said:

"I'm next door—you know that, of course. I'm sorry if you thing I'm being intrusive, but it obvious what is expected of us."

"But of course."

Fenella spoke shyly and felt hurt by something hard and slightly harsh in his tone.

"If you want to lock the door the key is on your side."

Again she felt as if he bruised her and in self-defence her voice became as indifferent as his.

"Thank you, I prefer to trust you."

"That's all right, then. Good night."

"Good night."

She merely whispered the words, but he had not waited for her reply; he limped across the room and was gone, the door of the dressing-room closing behind him with a sharp click.

She undressed slowly, hardly conscious of her actions so concentrated was she on her thoughts and feelings.

Had she been right or wrong to marry Nicholas?— that was the provoking question which presented itself over and over again—and having married him, what was the best way to face the future with him?

'He's a complete stranger to me,' Fenella thought.

She got into bed, slipping between the cool sheets, then lay looking at the closed door which divided them. Somehow, when she had gone to her wedding that morning it had been in a very different mood.

She had been desperate then for protection, for help of any sort which would relieve her anxiety and fear. She had believed that Nicholas would be a true friend, someone who would stand as a bulwark between herself and the world.

Now she was not so certain that she could use Nicholas in such a way. This morning he had seemed to have no personality of his own, the need of him had been entirely subsidiary to herself.

Now she was conscious of Nicholas as a person. He, too, had feelings and she could become aware of them by a change in the tone of his voice. Her imaginary picture of him had not been a true one, Fenella told herself, and it was all bewildering and rather frightening.

'I'm completely alone,' she thought.

Then suddenly the tears began flowing down her cheeks and she abandoned herself to her own misery which had been kept in check for so long.

In the long hours of the night Nicholas had seemed very formidable, but when she ran down the steps from the front door to where he was waiting for her in his car Fenella wondered why she had been so absurd.

He was smiling at her and there was something definitely boyish and confiding both in his smile and in the hand he held out in greeting.

"Well done! You're the only woman I've ever met who could really get dressed in fifteen minutes. I was preparing myself to wait at least another half an hour."

Fenella laughed.

"I expect the women you've known before have taken more trouble with themselves," she said. "I didn't waste much time titivating."

"I think you're fishing for a compliment," Nicholas said, "so I shan't play."

"I wasn't, as it happened," Fenella answered; "but I don't expect you to believe me."

"I shall always believe you," Nicholas said, suddenly serious. "So far I have found you to be a most truthful person."

"Thank you," Fenella replied.

They were silent as the car turned on to the main road.

It was a warm sunny day; the wind caught Fenella's hair and blew it back from her forehead. She felt as if it blew away many of the troubles and fears which had been upsetting her.

'Why should I worry so much?' she asked herself. 'Nicholas will look after us now and that leaves only Simon to fend for himself.'

She wondered how they were all going to get along in the future and then light-heartedly decided that she could let the future take care of itself. Impulsively she spoke her thoughts.

"You are being awfully kind, Nick. I am grateful—I am really."

"What have I done now?" he asked.

She realized that her remark was apropos of nothing that had been spoken aloud.

"Well—just everything," she said vaguely.

"I haven't begun yet," he said. "I want to be kind to you, Fenella, but you'll have to help me. I told you I was very inexperienced about women."

131

"Haven't you ever been in love?"

"Yes, once. I was nineteen and she was twenty-eight."

"And wouldn't she marry you?"

"She was married already. She made me very happy and extremely miserable. I'm certain it was all very educative, but it was an experience I would prefer not to repeat."

"No one else?" Fenella asked.

"No one else," he replied. "The war interfered with my social activities, as you might imagine."

"Of course." Fenella spoke gently.

The thought of the injuries Nicholas had suffered always moved her to a deep compassion.

Nicholas suddenly drew up the car.

"There's my agent," he exclaimed. "Do you mind if we speak to him a moment?"

A man on a big chestnut horse came galloping along the side of the road to them.

"Good morning, Nicholas," he said. "Congratulations. Your mother told me the news early this morning on the telephone."

"Thank you, Charles. I don't think you've met my wife," Nicholas replied. "Fenella, this is Charles Carstairs. He looks after the estate—hence its perfection."

"Thank you for those few kind words."

Charles Carstairs dismounted and shook hands with Fenella. He was a man of about fifty with a weather-beaten face and an engaging manner which made Fenella take to him at once.

"You must bring your wife over one evening. I've got something special put by in which to drink your health."

"We'll be there," Nicholas promised; "and, by the way, did Mother mention sending the van over to Four Gables for the luggage?"

"She did and it will be arriving about noon."

"Good."

"By the way, Lady Coleby," Charles Carstairs said, speaking to Fenella, "if you want a tenant for Four Gables let me know—I daresay I shall be able to find one, but I understand you are shutting it up for the moment."

"I think that will be best until we can make proper plans. But I'll talk to my Father about it this morning."

"I hear Major Ransome has found a billet the other side of the village," Carstairs went on. "A farmer called Scott has taken him in.

"I'm sorry that you had to have him in the first place. I've known Rex Ransome since he was a boy and he's always been somewhat of a bounder, especially where women are concerned."

Fenella gave a little gasp and then before she could speak she felt Nicholas's hand on hers and knew by the hard pressure of his fingers that he was entreating her not to reply.

"We must be off, Charles," he said. "See you this evening, I expect."

"I shall be up at the Court," Charles Carstairs replied, and raised his whip in salute as the car moved off.

Fenella said nothing until they turned into the gate at Four Gables. Then:

"Why should he say that?" The words seemed to burst from her lips.

"I'm afraid he is only voicing local opinion," Nicholas replied. He spoke slowly and obviously choosing his words with care.

"We know how much that's worth," Fenella said scornfully.

"Exactly."

"How dare people say such things when they don't understand, don't know what a man has suffered?" Fenella said aloud.

Nicholas did not answer and as they drew up at the front door she fancied he was frowning.

There was so much to do in the next hour or so that Fenella had no time to think of the agent's words or, indeed, of Rex himself. To begin with she found that her father had suddenly taken up an entirely contrary attitude about everything.

When she arrived he had just announced that he

133

would not give his consent to the children going to Wetherby Court and what was more he would not have the house shut up.

"Where am I going to go when I'm on leave?" he asked.

"You can't come here if there are no servants," Raymond said patiently. "Fenella's done all the work for you up to now and you can hardly expect Moo and Nannie to run the house without help."

"Well, get help then," Simon bellowed.

"They tell me that's impossible," Raymond said. "You don't seem to realize that there isn't a domestic of any sort to be had in this part of the world. Those who aren't in factories are working on the land."

"We shall be delighted if you will come and stay with us," Nicholas suggested.

"I don't want to stay with anyone," Simon said ungraciously. "I want my own home. Surely a man's entitled to that?"

"Now, Daddy, don't be difficult," Fenella said. "Let's leave things as they are at the moment."

● ● ●

At the railway station Fenella clung to Raymond.

"I wish you weren't going," she whispered.

"Now don't you worry," he admonished her, patting her on the shoulder. "Everything is going to be all right; and I like Nicholas, so be kind to him. The man's a fool to marry you, but that's his look-out."

Raymond gave his sister an affectionate hug, then he added in a very different voice:

"If anything happens, you'd better wire me. I'll try to come at once if it's humanly possible."

Fenella knew he referred to Elaine and she nodded, finding it almost impossible to speak now that Raymond was leaving.

It was with eyes misty with tears that she watched his train out of the station; then Moo's arm through hers she walked back to the car where Nicholas was waiting for them.

The whole party, Simon, Nannie, the children and

134

Moo, arrived at Wetherby Court just before luncheon. Fenella and Nicholas had persuaded Simon to go over with them, promising to arrange that the car should take him to the station in time to catch his train.

"What are you thinking of, Fenella?" Nicholas asked her suddenly.

"I was thinking that geniuses like Father should only have sons to bring up," Fenella answered.

"Most women are a damned nuisance," Simon said. "At the same time we couldn't do without them. They bring a great deal of colour into our lives."

"Too much sometimes," Lady Coleby said acidly.

But Simon, quite unabashed and irrepressible, answered:

"But still we, or shall I say I? can't do without them."

When Simon had gone, Lady Coleby said to Fenella:

"I think your Father is a most interesting man. The pity is that he has no one to look after him."

Fenella understood that she was not referring to Simon's material needs.

"No one has managed to do that since my mother died."

"It's a pity," Lady Coleby said, "a great pity."

Greatly daring, Fenella said:

"I wish you hadn't disapproved of Father all these years. It's prevented him as well as us from knowing a lot of people in the county who might have been friendly, who might have given him different interests."

Lady Coleby looked at Fenella coldly.

"I still disapprove of your Father, my dear," she said, "but it is no longer in my power to refuse to know him."

Fenella felt herself snubbed, at the same time she could not help being convinced that Simon's charms had managed once again to over-ride even Lady Coleby's scruples as regards his morals.

'There's something in Simon,' she thought, 'which defeats them all when they come in personal contact with him.'

Smiling a little at the thought, she ran upstairs to

find out how the children were settling into their new nursery.

● ● ●

"Fenella, I want to talk to you."

Nicholas came into the library where Fenella was busy finishing a letter to Raymond. She looked up from the writing-desk, her eyes preoccupied for the moment with her own thoughts.

"Yes?"

"I want to talk to you," Nicholas repeated, "about your war work."

He sat down in a chair beside her and now Fenella put down her pen and gave him her whole attention.

"About my war work?" she echoed.

"Yes. Raymond spoke to me about it before he left."

"He said something to me. The trouble is, Nicholas, what am I to do?"

"That's what I've been seeing about," Nicholas said, "and incidentally it's a long story which concerns myself."

"Tell me," Fenella commanded, leaning forward, her elbows on the desk, her face cupped in her hands.

"Well, it's like this," Nicholas began, hesitating and stammering a little over his words as he usually did when he was shy or embarrassed about what he had to say.

"Just before the war I was extremely keen on flying and after a good deal of argument I persuaded my Mother to let me build a private airfield about a mile from this house.

"I had the idea of starting a kind of club among my friends so that we could fly over to call on each other and also have a repair shop here where we could get our own machines attended to quickly and with the least amount of trouble.

"But before I'd gone very far, the war started and that finished everything as far as I was concerned; but the Air Ministry, in need of aerodromes, took an interest in the particular piece of land that had been levelled and prepared, and while they were doing so a cousin

136

of mine, Dick Brawn, asked if he could take charge of the sheds for some particular experiment he was doing in aviation.

"To cut a long story short, the place was considerably extended and Dick is at present working on a particular type of night-fighter which the Air Ministry hope will prove to be far better than anything else the R.A.F. have had up till now."

"And all this is going on here?" Fenella said. "How exciting! I'd no idea."

"Very few people have," Nicholas replied. "We've naturally kept very quiet about it although actually there are over a hundred people employed in the workshops. About half of these are local."

"Shall I be allowed to go over the aerodome?"

"That's just what I was going to talk to you about. You see, Fenella, it's like this. When I was so ill I had very little to think about and I began to work out in my own way what I thought would be certain improvements in an aeroplane from a pilot's point of view. Well, Dick is incorporating these in the new machine."

"Oh Nick, how thrilling!"

"You can imagine how I shall feel if it's successful, and"—here Nicholas looked rather shy—"Dick has been kind enough to consider my suggestions of such value that we have chosen a special name for the aeroplane."

"What is it?"

"The Cobra. It is, of course, the first letters of both our surnames."

"When will the Cobra be finished?"

"Actually in a few weeks, perhaps sooner; then the tests will be made. But this diverges from what I really came to tell you. I've been to see Dick this morning and he's perfectly willing, if you care to undertake it, to give you a job in the workshop."

"You mean that I can do my war work in your own factory," Fenella said.

"That's what it amounts to," Nicholas answered; "but of course you will be treated like every other hand and

137

I'm afraid it's unskilled labour and not very exciting at that."

"But I should love it! It's a marvellous idea of yours, and I should be much happier doing that than being in a post of responsibility. That's what I was afraid of getting as your wife."

"Well, the fact that you are my wife won't give you any pull where Dick's concerned," Nicholas said. "He's the fairest man I've ever met and what's more he's absolutely brilliant at his job. I think you'll like him, Fenella."

"When can I meet him?"

"I've arranged to take you to the aerodrome this afternoon."

"That'll be lovely," Fenella replied. "I only hope I shan't let you down."

"There's no fear of that," Nicholas said confidently.

But as he escorted Fenella through the workshops a few hours later she felt that this confidence was unjustified.

The men and women all seemed to her to be working swiftly and competently; she watched their hands moving ceaselessly to and fro, the flash of the tools they used, their air of assurance, and felt herself absolutely lacking in all that made a good workman.

She was, however, slightly reassured when she met Dick Brawn, for she felt that Nicholas had been entirely right when he had said that being his wife would not give her any particular pull where his cousin was concerned.

'If he doesn't think I'm good enough he'll ask me to go,' she thought and was somewhat comforted.

She liked Dick Brawn although she was frightened of him. He was a short, stout man with a bullet head and large horn-rimmed glasses which give him an owl-like expression.

He spoke quickly and forcefully and one's immediate impression was of someone forceful, dynamic, yet capable to a certain extent of controlling his own personality when there were wider issues than his own at stake.

Fenella liked him and had the idea that he liked her too.

She had half suspected that Dick Brawn might have incorporated Nicholas's ideas out of sentimental affection for his injured cousin.

It would have been easy for him to help Nicholas's recovery by giving him something to think about, by occupying his mind.

But having seen Nicholas in the factory and with Dick Brawn, Fenella knew with absolute certainty that affection or sentiment had nothing to do with their relationship in business.

Nicholas played his part because of his ability and she looked at her husband with new eyes, seeing in this environment a personality far removed from the stammering, hesitant young man whom she had known up to date.

She watched him as he pored over blueprints with Dick Brawn, she saw him as they inspected the big aeroplane engine, she heard him speaking to the workmen and saw a very different Nicholas indeed.

He was a man cool and calm, used to authority, ready to give the right answer to a question, not assuming leadership but being by instinct a leader among men.

On the airfield itself there were various aircraftsmen and a small party of officers who had flown down that day to see Dick. With them, Fenella noticed, Nicholas showed no signs of shyness.

Most of them seemed to know him well and to like him, while every one of the ground staff had a cheery word for him and she remarked that more than once Nicholas stopped to ask a man about his personal affairs.

'How he must hate being out of the Air Force!' was her first reaction to all this.

She wondered if even his new work here was enough compensation for being deprived of the life he must have enjoyed so tremendously.

They spent nearly the whole afternoon on the aerodrome and then Fenella was given her orders for nine o'clock the next morning.

"Do you think I shall ever be able to do the work they want properly?" she asked Nicholas as they drove home.

"I'm quite certain you will," he answered. "Don't get worried. The foreman will take you in hand."

"You don't think the other work people will dislike me? They might think I was spying on them on your behalf or Dick's."

"I should think it most unlikely. They all love Dick, but I should go canny, as they say, to start with."

"I'll do that all right."

"I hate your doing this really," Nicholas said suddenly as they drove along the narrow tree-bordered lane which led them back to the Court.

"Why?" Fenella asked in surprise.

"I don't suppose any man enjoys seeing his wife go to work," Nicholas replied. "It strikes pretty hard at our manhood. But it's infinitely worse when one is unable to work oneself."

"But you do," Fenella expostulated. "You heard what Dick said to me to-day and, Nick, I think it's wonderful what you should have invented anything so important as the Cobra."

She spoke hesitantly, half afraid of seeming too gushing, a little shy of expressing her appreciation of her husband.

"Thank you," Nicholas spoke softly, then he added: "By the way, don't talk about this, will you? Not even to Mother."

"She knows, of course?"

"Not as much as you do. She knows I mess about down there, naturally, but she doesn't know yet that I've an actual hand in the invention of the Cobra—in fact, she knows nothing about the aeroplane at all."

Fenella felt suddenly very glad. It was mean of her, she knew, and yet she couldn't help being delighted at being in one thing at least put in front of her dominating mother-in-law.

"Fenella," he asked after a moment, "are you any happier?"

Fenella forced the answer between her lips even while her heart cried out it was a lie.

"Much happier, Nicholas."

"Good. And you are glad you married me?"

This time it was impossible to answer him, she couldn't force herself to give him the reply he wanted.

Instead, Fenella looked ahead to where the many-paned windows of the house were shimmering in the afternoon sun.

"Must we talk about it?"

"Why not?" Nicholas asked the question abruptly and Fenella fancied there was an angry note in his voice. "Aren't we modern enough to discuss anything and everything? I thought it went out of fashion years ago to have repressions."

Fenella tried to laugh lightly, but the sound was a failure; her voice broke and to her own horror she was aware of the tears flowing from her eyes down her face.

Nicholas stopped the car, he switched off the engine and turned round in his seat to face her.

"Fenella," he said, "look at me."

She didn't obey him, and he put out his hand and taking her by the shoulder turned her round so that she must look at him.

"Why must you be so abominably obstinate?" he asked angrily.

"Obstinate!" Fenella echoed the word in surprise and her tears stopped automatically.

"Yes, obstinate," Nicholas repeated. "You want to like me—you do like me, and if you were honest with yourself you'd admit that there are things of interest and enjoyment in being married to me; but instead of being frank and truthful you prefer to cling to your own ridiculous fancies. What do you know of love—a child like you?"

Fenella felt herself quail before the anger in his voice, then proudly she raised her head.

"My love is a very real thing."

"I wonder?" Nicholas asked. "Wasn't it just an affair of kisses and moonlight, of being swept off your feet because you were so young and so damnably innocent?"

"You're making me hate you," Fenella said fiercely.

"Good—at least I'm raising some emotion in you. Oh, what's the use!"

Nicholas let her go suddenly, he started the car and without another word drove up the drive. Fenella felt her senses reeling. This couldn't be true, Nicholas speaking to her like this, Nicholas fierce, angry and disturbing.

Here was another aspect of the man she had married—a man who could frighten and disturb her—where she had expected a boy soft and pliable.

The car stopped at the front door. Fenella turned towards her husband

"Nicholas," she said pleadingly.

But he did not look at her; he was frowning and she knew that his eyes were dark.

"There's nothing more to say," he said crossly; "words don't help. You'd better get out and go in."

Meekly she turned and obeyed him.

The following day Fenella started work. She felt nervous as she arrived at the factory, but the foreman, a genial man who told Fenella that he had started work as a child of twelve, showed her what to do and assured her it would come easy enough after the first day or two.

Later as she lay in a hot bath soaking herself luxuriously, she thought of the people who had to go back to squalid little billets or to overcrowded homes where they often had to turn to and do a bit of housework.

'I won't let Nicholas down,' she thought.

She was surprised that Nicholas should be uppermost in her mind, and yet all the time she was working she had found herself thinking of his fighter, of the Cobra.

More than once since she had come to his home some indirect reference to his injuries or some half-suppressed regret of what he could not do had made

Fenella ashamed that up till now the war had affected her so very little.

It was hard to watch Nicholas struggle from the seat of a car or get up awkwardly from the table without wanting to help him.

Some days he walked better than others, but at times he seemed almost to have lost control of his feet so that they slipped and slithered away from him and he must grip the furniture for support.

Fenella knew, too, that often he spent long sleepless nights when the pain of his wounds would not let him rest, and she had learned as well from Lady Coleby that there was every chance he would have to be operated on again in the near future.

"That will be five operations," Nicholas's mother said, and added: "Poor boy, he has been very brave about them."

Ever since she had been a child Fenella had shrunk from physical suffering and now when she thought of Nicholas and watched him she felt as if his pain had an echo within herself.

She felt like that when Lady Coleby referred to her son's injuries in that calm, impersonal voice as if she spoke of something which happened to a stranger, and she was horrified once when she entered a room unexpectedly to hear Moo asking Nicholas if she could see his wounds.

"How can you ask such a thing!" Fenella had said fiercely to her younger sister.

She spoke all the more angrily and heatedly because within herself she felt the reproach that she—Nicholas's wife—could not bear to see them.

"But I'm interested," Moo said in surprise. "Nicholas has been telling me of the things that have been done to him, and if the war goes on long enough I shall be a nurse. No factories for me."

"You'd hate nursing," Fenella said scornfully. "Besides, you'd be no good at it."

There was some strange instinct within herself which wanted to be unkind, almost cruel to Moo.

"How do you know?" Moo riposted. "I haven't had a chance to be good at anything yet."

"That's true enough," Nicholas said. "And if you want a chance you shall have it, Moo."

"Thank you, Nickie, you're a darling."

Moo slipped her arm through her brother-in-law's, snuggling against him. Fenella felt her anger rising.

"Moo, will you go upstairs and say I want to see the children? Ask Nannie to bring them down."

Moo got slowly to her feet.

"I bet it's only an excuse to get rid of me."

"Will you please do what you're told," Fenella commanded.

Moo went out of the room and slammed the door behind her. Fenella turned to Nicholas.

"I don't think it's good for Moo to be promised everything she asks for," she said. "Or is it your way of gaining a cheap popularity?"

There was an edge on her voice as she spoke and Nicholas got slowly to his feet.

"What's the matter, Fenella?"

"Nothing," Fenella said snappily, and yet had she wished she could have told him what was the matter.

She had felt a moment of utter loneliness when she had seen Moo with her arm through Nicholas's snuggling against him.

They had looked so cosy, so happy together that Fenella had felt out of it, alien to their interests and utterly lonely with her own aching desires and unhappiness.

Now, ashamed of herself, ashamed of the emotion she could not control, she turned towards the door.

"Come back, Fenella," Nicholas called, but she hurried away from him, knowing that he could not catch her.

That little scene returned over and over again to disturb her. She reconstructed it in her mind as she worked. That and many other little incidents continued to haunt her.

'Why am I so unkind, so beastly?' she asked herself,

and yet could find no answer to act as palliative to her own restlessness.

It was impossible to excuse herself completely on the ground that she was still worried and anxious; there were deeper emotions than that flowing beneath the surface of her anxiety about Elaine and the trivial difficulties and irritations of living at Wetherby Court.

There was Rex and there was Nicholas, warring with each other within her thoughts, tearing her, it seemed to her sometimes, apart in her desire only to find some peace within herself where neither of them could hurt her.

As she stood alone in her bedroom one night after she had been at work in the factory for nearly a week, Fenella asked herself exactly how much her present mode of life meant to her.

It seemed to her that a voice which was not her own and yet was part of her answered:

"You are alone, utterly alone—but whose fault is that?"

CHAPTER SIX

Moo burst into Fenella's bedroom.

"You're wanted on the telephone."

"Who is it?" Fenella asked irritably, looking up from the dressing-table where she was putting the finishing touches to her hair. "I'm late as it is."

"It's someone speaking for Simon," Moo replied. "The line's rather indistinct but they said they must speak to you—it's urgent."

"He can't be coming on leave again!" Fenella exclaimed, putting down her comb and getting to her feet. "Get my coat out for me, there's an angel, and I want a clean handkerchief."

She hurried out of the room and ran downstairs to the morning-room. It was always a scramble to get off to the factory in the morning and she resented anything which made her late.

She picked up the telephone receiver from the writing-table.

"Hello?"

"Hello. Is that Lady Coleby?"

"Yes, I'm speaking."

It was a man's voice who questioned her, and then as Fenella listened and grew attuned to his calm, impersonal tone and heard what he had to say she groped for the writing-chair.

146

What she was hearing couldn't be true—it couldn't be, she kept thinking to herself, and yet the quiet voice went on.

Finally, when she replaced the receiver she sat for a moment staring into space, then got to her feet and looked round her almost wildly as if she hardly knew what to do—where to begin the task which lay ahead of her.

"Moo! Nicholas!" She called their names from the bottom of the stairs, then ran up to them, breathless and panting by the time she reached her bedroom.

"What's the matter?" Moo saw her face before she could speak and ran across the room.

"Nicholas! Nick—come here, I want you."

It was a cry almost of desperation and Nicholas threw open the communicating door between their bedrooms. He was in his shirt-sleeves with a hairbrush in his hand.

"What's happened?"

"It's Simon," Fenella gasped.

"What's happened to him?—tell us what's happened?" Moo pleaded.

"Its . . oh! I can't say it."

Fenella gave a little sobbing cry and Moo's arms were round her, holding her close.

"Don't, Fenella, don't!" she pleaded; while Nicholas, supporting his unsteady footsteps against the furniture, reached her and put a comforting hand on her shoulder.

"Take it easy, Fenella," he said soothingly.

"I'm all right, it's just the shock I think," Fenella whispered. "I can't imagine anything happening to Father."

"What has happened?" Moo asked.

Fenella raised her head and looked at her with wide eyes; then slowly, in a voice of horror, she spoke the words.

"Simon is blind."

"Blind! Why? Has there been an accident?"

It was Nicholas who asked the question, for Moo could only stare at her sister.

"It's some sort of poisoning," Fenella explained. "At

147

least, that's what the doctor thinks. He said Simon has contracted a rare and almost unknown disease of the eyes. They believe, although they aren't sure, that it started from some paint he has been using.

"In a young person or someone whose eyes are normally strong there would be no reason to expect that the disease would prove fatal to the sight, but Simon's eyes apparently were in a bad state.

"I remember now that he complained about them when he was at home; he told me that they ached, but was furious when I suggested that he ought to go to an oculist, said it would make him feel old if he had to wear glasses."

"But when did this happen?" Nicholas asked

"Apparently he has been under treatment for over a fortnight," Fenella answered. "It's so like Simon not to tell them to notify us. But now the specialist wants him to rest for some weeks before they do anything further and he insists on coming hime."

"Home!" Moo echoed.

"Yes, home to Four Gables. Apparently he wants more than anything else to be in a place that he knows. I can understand it, of course, and he's arriving to-day."

"But he can't go there alone."

"Of course not," Fenella replied. "I must go over at once and open up the house for him. You'd better come too and help me."

"Wouldn't he come here?" Nicholas asked.

Fenella shook her head.

"I suggested that to the doctor, but he said Simon had only one fixed idea in his mind and that was to be in familiar surroundings. The doctor thinks it might be advantageous to do what he wishes.

"They are sending a nurse with him, of course, not that she'll be much help in the house if I know anything of nurses."

"Better take one of the maids from here over with you," Nicholas suggested.

"Can I?" Fenella looked up at him gratefully. "That would be a help. And Nick, will you explain to the factory and get me leave of absence or whatever it's called?"

"Of course I will, and you'll want to go over to Four Gables right away, won't you? What time is your Father arriving?"

"At lunch-time." Fenella got to her feet. "I can't think for a moment what I shall want. Moo, darling, go and pack some of your own things and then come and help me."

"All right." Moo went to the door.

But as they reached it turned back.

"Fenella," she asked in a whisper, "will he really be blind for always?"

"They don't know," Fenella replied. "We can only hope that it's not as bad as they fear. After all, Simon is an amazingly resilient person."

Moo still hesitated.

"I think I'm afraid of seeing him like that. One can't imagine Daddy being helpless."

Fenella said nothing and after a moment Moo went out of the room and shut the door behind her.

Fenella realized that Nicholas was still with her.

"I feel rather like Moo," she said. "I, too, am afraid."

"It's a ghastly thing," he answered; "but perhaps it isn't as bad as they anticipate."

"The doctor sounded pretty definite. Oh, Nick, what a tragic thing for Simon of all people!"

"I'm desperately sorry about it," Nicholas answered, "and you know I want to help."

"There was a pause, then he added:

"May I come to Four Gables with you?"

The question caught Fenella unawares and for a moment she was confused, unable to find words in which to answer him. Then not looking at him moving the things on her dressing-table aimlessly, she replied:

"You'd be awfully uncomfortable. I think it would be better if Moo and I went alone. After all, you can come over and see us, can't you."

149

"Yes, I can come over and see you," Nicholas echoed.

Fenella fancied there was a faint touch of sarcasm in his voice.

'Shall I let him come? Shall I ask him to stay with us at Four Gables?' she debated within herself, but before she could find an answer the door of Nicholas' dressing-room closed softly and she was alone.

She had no time in the hours that followed to think either of her own feelings or of those of Nicholas.

There was a great deal to do; and while both Moo and the maid they took from Wetherby Court to Four Gables worked willingly enough, it was left to Fenella to make all the arrangements and do most of the preparations before her Father's arrival.

When the moment arrived to go to the station and meet Simon, Fenella felt as if she was so exhausted she had no energy left for the emotional meeting which lay before her. She felt almost faint as the train appeared.

As she watched it coming nearer and nearer towards them she felt Moo's hand slip into hers and knew that the child was tense with fear and anticipation.

She gave Moo's fingers a reassuring squeeze, hoping that she herself looked braver than she felt.

'I've got to be sensible,' she thought, and wished she had let Nicholas come with them.

Instead, after he had dropped them at Four Gables she had said good-bye to him abruptly.

'I would like his support now,' she thought.

She regretted the impulse which had made her insist to herself that this was entirely a family affair. After all, Nicholas, legally at any rate, was one of the family.

But it was too late for regrets. The train drew into the station and Fenella and Moo stood looking at the passengers as they alighted until at last they saw their Father.

He was in uniform, wearing black glasses, and was being helped out of the carriage by a young woman dressed in nurses' uniform. They hurried towards him and felt a great relief when they heard his voice in loud and what appeared to be quite normal tones saying gruffly:

"Now you haven't told me how big a drop I've got. Not that you ever could judge distance."

"It's about a foot and a half," the nurse replied. "Steady now."

Simon, holding on to her arm, lowered himself on to the platform; but he moved forward too quickly, nearly knocking down a porter.

"The place is full of people," he grumbled.

Fenella put out her hand to touch him.

"Simon, here we are."

"Is that you, Fenella?" he asked. "So you've come to meet me. Anyone with you?"

"Yes, me—Moo."

"Good heavens, girl, where's your grammar? Here, give me your arm, Fenella; I feel like a damned half-wit, groping my way about. Not that Nurse Bennett doesn't do her best. Now where's that woman got to?"

"I'm here," the nurse answered, "just at your elbow. I was seeing to our luggage."

Fenella held out her hand.

"How do you do? I'm Fenella Coleby and this is my sister."

Nurse Bennett smiled and they liked her immediately.

"I've heard a lot about you, Lady Coleby."

"Come on, come on, what are we waiting for?" Simon asked irritably. "I want to get home."

They led him to the taxi waiting outside. He had little to say on the homeward journey and both Fenella and Moo found it hard to talk naturally. Only Nurse Bennett was at her ease, while Simon seemed to enjoy the half-jovial, half-bullying manner she adopted towards him.

'He looks ill,' Fenella thought, noting how pale and shrunken his cheeks seemed.

"Where's that husband of yours?" Simon asked suddenly as they turned in at the drive gates. "Does he

151

mind your coming home to look after your poor old father?"

"I'm afraid I didn't ask him if he minded," Fenella replied. "We've been working like blacks the whole morning ever since we heard you were coming."

Simon turned his face in the direction of Nurse Bennett.

"You'll like my son-in-law," he said. "He's been spoilt by having too much of this world's goods, although that's an advantage when it comes to a question of marriage. All the same, rich or poor, I like him."

"He's got the most wonderful house in the world," Moo ejaculated enthusiastically. "We shall have to take Nurse over to see it, shan't we, Daddy? It's full of treasures, marvellous ones, and there's a priest's hidey-hole which was built in the fifteenth century."

"I've heard of Wetherby Court," Nurse said. "It sounds a lovely place. I'd certainly like to see it."

"I shan't be able to spare you," Simon interjected. "What do you imagine you are going to with me on your day out? Tie me up like a dog until you return?"

"You'll soon get used to looking after yourself," Nurse Bennett said firmly.

The home-coming was easier than Fenella had anticipated, and yet when finally they had got Simon unpacked and changed into civilian clothes it seemed to Fenella that he had altered a good deal from the swaggering, blustering Simon she had known on his last leave.

However, she did not have long to think about him as Rex had heard she had returned home and had called to see her to try and persuade her to go away with him.

But of course she had refused knowing she could not let her family down or could she?

Wearily, Fenella felt the old familiar questions closing in around her, haunting her, taunting her with their queries to which she could find no satisfactory answer.

She heard the door open and turned towards it eagerly, wanting to escape from herself, from her own thoughts.

She expected to see Moo or Nurse Bennett, but it was Nicholas who came into the room leaning on his stick.

"Hello," Fenella said, "I wasn't expecting to see you so early."

"Perhaps it's a good thing I didn't come any earlier," he retorted.

She knew that he must have seen Rex leaving the house. She felt her anger rise at the harsh, peremptory note in his voice.

"If by that you mean that you've met Rex Ransome," she said, "he came to say good-bye. He's going out East."

"So he told me. Why did he want to see you?"

"I've told you," Fenella answered, "to say good-bye."

Nicholas walked to the fire-place and putting down his stick steadied himself against the mantelpiece.

"Fenella," he said, "I'm not being unreasonable, but you can't trust that chap. I've heard a lot of stories about him lately and they're not particularly pleasant ones."

"I shouldn't bother to repeat them to me," Fenella replied. "As you know, I'm very fond of Rex and nothing you could say against him would be likely to prejudice me."

She tried to speak steadily, but the colour rose in her cheeks and the words came from between lips that were trembling.

"Are you so dense that you can't understand the type of man he is?" Nicholas asked. "He's a womaniser. He's run after every woman in this neighbourhood for years and now when he meets anyone as young and fresh as you of course he tells you that you're the love of his life."

"Isn't it the same old story that every village maiden falls for."

"I won't listen to you—I won't," Fenella said, stamping her foot. "I didn't think you were so petty-minded, so stupid as to be degradingly jealous."

"All right then, I am jealous," Nick replied. "I admit it; but haven't I every reason to be?

"Ever since you married me you've mooned about the place with a miserable expression because you love this man Ransome, and now the very first time that you leave my roof I find him sneaking out of here."

"He came to say good-bye. It was not a pre-arranged meeting," Fenella said proudly.

"I believe you, but I don't trust him and I won't have him hanging about you."

"He's not likely to do that. I'm not going to see him again."

Fenella spoke without anger, for suddenly she felt how fruitless this whole argument was. Rex gone from her life for ever . . Nicholas hurt and jealous.

'I'm not worth all this unhappiness, this misery,' she thought.

She felt a surging revolt within her against everything, against the trials and difficulties which seemed insurmountable, against herself and all the feelings warring within her over which she had no control.

She looked at Nicholas and felt that he, too, was bewildered and made miserable by the things which happened beyond his control. He had been hurt physically and now she was dealing him mental blows.

There was Simon alone in the darkness . . there was Elaine holding on to life by some strange strength which would not release her tortured spirit . . and yet in the midst of so many real tragedies there was her own petty, insignificant unhappiness, her longing for a man who could not be hers, her desire for any kind of life rather than the one which she had to live.

'How hopeless we are,' Fenella thought to herself, 'so contrary, so unstable. Is it any wonder there are wars when human beings are never at peace within themselves?'

She turned towards Nicholas impulsively.

"I'm sorry, Nick, I've been a fool about many things. Can't we forget it?"

He looked at her, but she saw no hope dawn in his expression. It was as if he did not understand her.

"It isn't a question of forgetting," he said. "I wish there was more to remember."

She was about to answer him when the door opened and Moo came in. For once Fenella was not glad of the interruption.

Usually she welcomed her younger sister breaking up any tête-à-tête between herself and Nicholas, for she always felt a little ill at ease with him, a little apprehensive in case they should plunge into conversational and emotional depths in which she became unsure of herself.

Now the thought came to her, as Moo came across the room chattering gaily of her shopping expedition, that Nicholas's friendship was the one thing which she must not lose.

In the past weeks she had clung inflexibly to her love for Rex. Now, finally, he was gone from her life and she knew that she must force herself not to think of him, to let him go from her mind as ruthlessly as she had let him go from the house.

She had been strong enough to resist his desire for her, she had found strength enough to deny a happiness which must be bought at too great a cost.

Now she must have strength enough to control the treachery of her body which still needed him, of her mind which must continually look backwards into the past.

"I can't tell you how nice everyone was to me," Moo was saying. "Everyone asked about Daddy, and what do you think, Fenella?—Mrs. Hooper actually suggested that if we wanted any fruit she could spare us a few greengages."

Fenella was just about to answer when Moo, looking from her to Nicholas, said:

"What's the matter with you two? You both look queer. You've not been fighting, have you?"

"Of course not," Fenella said.

But she didn't sound entirely convincing, and Moo, slipping her arm through Nicholas's, said:

"I think you're both ridiculous. You're the two nicest people in the world—I can't think what you find that's worth quarrelling about."

Nicholas bent down and kissed his sister-in-law's cheek.

"The trouble is, Moo," he said, "I ought to have waited for you to grow up. You'd have appreciated me. Unfortunately, I'm not Fenella's idea of an ideal husband."

He spoke bitterly and Fenella knew he was deeply hurt, but she felt it was impossible for her to attempt to find words in which to placate him.

She picked up the parcels which Moo had put down on the table and walked towards the door.

"I'll put these in the kitchen," she said, but neither Nicholas nor Moo answered her.

She helped the maid from Wetherby Court get the tea ready and as a sop to a pricking conscience cut some specially nice sandwiches, but when she went back to the sitting-room it was to find Moo there alone.

"Where's Nicholas?" she asked.

"He's gone home," Moo replied.

The child was sitting in the window-seat, an open book on her knee, but Fenella was aware as she entered that Moo had not been reading. Now she got down, the book falling to the floor with a thud.

She came across the room to Fenella, then speaking in a voice hardly above a whisper she said:

"Fenella, he's terribly unhappy."

"Who is?" Fenella enquired, although she knew the answer.

"Nicholas. Oh, why are you so unkind to him?"

"I don't think I can discuss this with you," Fenella said awkwardly.

She was arranging the teaspoons and not looking at her sister as she spoke.

"Why can't you discuss it with me?" Moo asked. "We always have talked about things, you and I, but now you are shutting me out just as you are shutting him out too.

"You're not happy, Fenella, I know that; I've known it ever since you got married; but he loves you and no one could be nicer than Nick. Why don't you love him?"

Fenella straightened her back.

"I don't know; one can't command love."

"But one can grow to love people," Moo insisted. "One does grow to love them. Once you get to know them well, to understand all the nice inside things about them, you begin to feel warm and affectionate towards them . . fond and . . oh, I can't explain, but surely that's really loving a person, isn't it?"

"I don't know," Fenella said wearily.

"You loved Rex, didn't you?" Moo went on. "It all happened quickly and excitingly when you first met each other. I saw that. But, Fenella, you didn't know anything about him, you didn't become real friends with him like we have become friends with Nicholas. How do you know that what you felt for Rex wasn't like . ."

She hesitated, and then the words came with a rush . .

"Like Daddy and Elaine?"

"Will you be quiet!" Fenella turned on her sister, angry now, her eyes blazing, her breath coming quickly. "How dare you say such things to me! What do you know about it? You're only a child!"

The quick tears sprang into Moo's eyes.

"I'm sorry, Fenella, I was only trying to understand. Nicholas was so unhappy and I saw Rex in the village."

"I can't discuss it, Moo," Fenella said in a calmer tone. "If you want to please me and to make me happy you'll not try to interfere."

"All right," Moo retorted, "but I like Nicholas, I love him even if you don't and one day you will be sorry."

The tears overflowed from her eyes and ran down her cheeks. With a little sob she turned towards the door.

"I think you're beastly to him," she said, then slammed the door behind her.

Fenella stood and tried metaphorically to shrug her shoulders. She knew that her cheeks were burning and there was something empty and aching within her heart.

Even Moo was against her now and she had no one to whom she could turn, no one who could show her any way out of this mass of complications in which she had got herself involved.

'I've a good mind to run away with Rex,' she thought savagely.

But she knew that her words were empty, there was no impulse within her to do anything of the sort.

Automatically she poured herself out a cup of tea, then heard footsteps coming across the hall before the door opened to admit Simon and Nurse Bennett. Simon was feeling his way with an outstretched hand.

"Don't help me," he commanded. "I know where everything is in this room unless some damned fool has moved it. Are you there, Fenella?"

"Yes, I'm here by the fire-place," Fenella replied, "and the tea's here, too."

"In its usual place?" Simon asked, advancing.

"In its usual place," she replied, taking up the cake-stand and moving it from his path.

He reached the corner of the sofa in safety, steered round it and lowered himself with caution.

"I did that well, didn't I?" he asked, as pleased as a small boy with his own progress.

"Your Father's the best patient I've ever had," Nurse Bennett said to Fenella. "The only trouble is he's a bit too venturesome."

"It always was one of my failings," Simon answered complacently.

The telephone rang sharply. Fenella got up to answer it. It was her mother-in-law. Fenella listened to what she had to say, gave an exclamation of surprise, then came back to the tea-table.

"Who was it?" Simon asked.

"Lady Coleby."

"What did she want?" Simon enquired without any great degree of interest in his voice.

"Oh, nothing very important," Fenella said. "I'll just get some more hot water."

Only Nurse Bennett saw that this was an excuse, the jug was already full, but she said nothing as Fenella left the room.

"Moo!" Fenella called as she got outside.

Moo answered her from the top landing.

"I'm just coming; is tea ready?"

"Come here quickly."

Moo came running down the stairs, the tell-tale marks of tears round her eyes.

"What do you think?" Fenella asked. "The most extraordinary thing has happened. Nicholas's mother has just rung up to say that someone has called there asking for me. 'A Miss McClelland', and she says that she is our Aunt.

"Lady Coleby has sent her on here, she'll be here at any moment. I haven't said anything to Daddy, I don't know what to say."

"That would be Aunt Julie," Moo exclaimed, and Fenella turned towards her in surprise.

"What do you mean—what do you know about this?"

Moo blushed.

"Raymond told me," she said, "but it was to be a secret from you. I didn't know, of course, she was going to turn up unexpectedly."

"Raymond told you what?" Fenella enquired.

"About Aunt Julie. She's our mother's sister, you know, and Raymond went to see her a week or so ago."

"Went to see her!" Fenella echoed. "But why? When did he tell you this?"

"Oh, Fenella, don't be angry," Moo pleaded, "but after you got married, before he went away I had a talk with him and I suggested that it would be so nice if our mother's relations took a little interest in us. You know how awful everything was then about Elaine and Daddy.

"Well, I told Raymond that I'd often thought of running away and he said

'Who to?'

'Well, we must have some relations somewhere,' I replied.

'By Jove! that's an idea,' he remarked. 'It's going to be a bit hard on Nicholas having you all on his hands.'

"Well, about ten days ago he wrote to me; said I wasn't to tell you anything as yet, but when his ship was in the West of Scotland he found himself quite near Mother's old home, so he went over and introduced himself and apparently our Aunt Julie was awfully nice to him.

"She said she'd come down to see you one day and ask if we couldn't be friends after all this time. Oh, Fenella, don't be cross!

"I know Raymond was afraid you'd think it was disloyal to Daddy. Of course he didn't know then anything was wrong with him and that he would be here. I do see what a muddle it all is."

"Muddle!" Fenella ejaculated, putting her hands to her forehead. "I can't think, I don't know what to do. She'll be arriving in a minute. Listen! isn't that the car now?"

It was a car and a moment later they heard it stop outside the front door.

"What shall we do?" Moo asked agitatedly.

Fenella forced herself to smile.

"Don't worry," she said.

She took Moo's hand in hers and walked firmly towards the front door. She opened it just as the woman outside raised her hand to the bell.

Fenella's first impression was that the newcomer hadn't the slightest resemblance to her Mother. She had forgotten, of course, that Arline would have aged considerably since Simon had painted the picture of her which was so linked with their childhood's memories.

Then Fenella realized that though the woman standing on the doorstep had grey hair, there was a likeness to their Mother in the dark blue eyes and the curve of the smiling mouth.

"How do you do?" the newcomer said shyly. "I think

160

Lady Coleby will have rung up to tell you that I was coming. My name is Julie McClelland."

"My mother-in-law did telephone," Fenella replied. "I am Fenella and this is Moo."

"I am sorry to turn up so unexpectedly," Miss McClelland said, "but Raymond assured me it was the best way. I'm not so certain now that he was right."

"Won't you come in?" Fenella asked.

She led the way into the empty studio, hoping that Simon would not hear their voices as they passed through the hall.

"What a lovely room!" Miss McClelland exclaimed, and then noting the easel added: "I suppose this is where your Father works? Lady Coleby said something was wrong with his eyes. I am sorry—is it really serious?"

"I'm afraid so," Fenella answered. "He's quite blind."

"Oh, what a ghastly tragedy!" Miss McClelland exclaimed.

"We still hope he may be cured," Fenella said.

"I hope so too," Julie McClelland said softly.

There was an awkward silence; then seating herself on the sofa Miss McClelland said:

"Perhaps I'd better start to explain myself from the beginning. I'm sure you are feeling as shy as I am, but it's all Raymond's fault that I didn't write to you first.

"You see, when he came to visit us and asked me to come down here to make your acquaintance he wasn't certain that you wouldn't refuse to meet me."

"How silly!" Fenella said impulsively.

"I don't know," Miss McClelland answered. "You see, I do appreciate that we—my family—are at fault. My Father was a very embittered man. I'm afraid he never forgave your Mother for marrying against his wishes.

"He was of the old school, proud and unbending; that sounds ridiculous in these days, doesn't it?"

"Is he dead?" Moo asked.

"Yes; he died last year, and my Mother died several

years ago. I'm the only one left—your only near relation on your Mother's side."

"Were you very surprised to see Raymond?" Moo enquired.

"Very surprised," Miss McClelland replied. "I didn't know who he was at first, but as soon as he began to talk I saw the family resemblance. You, of course, are very like your Mother."

She bent across to touch Fenella's hand as she spoke.

"I haven't got red hair."

"No, but your face is the same shape and you smile like her. Arline was a very lovely person, and I can't tell you how much I have missed her all these years."

"Why didn't you ever write to her?" Fenella asked.

"It seems silly to say that I was afraid, doesn't it?" her aunt replied; "but it is the truth. You see, although I was eight years older than Arline I had been brought up very strictly and very severely by my Father.

"In his way I'm afraid he was somewhat of a tyrant. We were hardly allowed to have a thought of our own that he hadn't approved first.

"But Arline was always independent, even when she was a tiny child, and because of her spirit I think he loved her the best of all his children. We had two brothers, but they were killed in the last war."

"Well, if he loved her so much . ." Moo began.

"That was why he minded her running away," Miss McClelland interposed. "You know if you love someone very much how easy it is for them to hurt you.

"He was both hurt and angry and therefore it was impossible for him ever to forgive her. But I think he missed her right up to his dying day."

"I wish I had known him," Moo said.

"I wish you had too," Aunt Julie said, "it might have made him very much happier if he had known his grandchildren; but, you see, you were never mentioned in his presence, we were never allowed to refer to you."

"It does seem funny, doesn't it?" Moo said.

Miss McClelland sighed.

"I suppose it does. I lived with it too long to have the

courage to challenge such a state of affairs. But I expect you think I am a very stupid person."

She smiled, and her smile brought back so many memories for Fenella that impulsively she held out her hand.

"We're very glad to know you now."

"You make me very happy when you say that," Aunt Julie replied, taking Fenella's hand in both of hers. "I don't think I have ever been more frightened than when I saw that large and lovely house of yours and wondered what sort of reception I'd get.

"Raymond was so nervous that you'd turn me away. He said you were a very sweet person, but also very loyal and very proud."

"I suppose I used to seem so," Fenella said, "but really I think we all longed to know our Mother's relations. I know when I was a child I used to wonder what you were like and wish I had lots of aunts and uncles to give me presents at Christmas and ask us to stay."

"You're making me feel very guilty," Aunt Julie said.

"How did you get here to-day?" Moo enquired.

"I have some friends in the Ministry of Information who had to visit Melchester."

"Oh, that's only about five miles from here," Fenella said.

"Yes, I know, and I got the local taxi to bring me out. It will wait till I return."

Moo looked at Fenella, and Fenella understood what her sister wished to say. She hesitated and then boldly took the plunge.

"Won't you stay now you are here? It won't be very comfortable, but we'll manage it somehow."

"May I?"—Aunt Julie flushed with pleasure. "I did hope you'd ask me. You see, although Raymond told me a lot about you, we have so very many years to catch up. I want to know everything and I want to see Timothy and Susan."

"Did he tell you about them too?" Moo asked.

"He told me a lot about them," Aunt Julie replied. "And I love children."

Fenella understood just how much her aunt wished to imply. She was trying to tell them that she was prepared to accept everything about them——Simon and his eccentricities, the children of his third marriage, all the scandal and unpleasantness which had surrounded their names for so many years.

It was indeed a supreme effort to bury the hatchet and Fenella felt the only thing they could do was to accept their Aunt Julie with open arms. The one difficulty which remained was Simon.

Fenella was wondering how best to approach her Father when to her horror the door opened and Simon came in holding Nurse Bennett by the arm.

"There's a picture in here I want to show you," he was saying.

They all got to their feet awkwardly.

"Oh, here you are," Nurse Bennett said brightly. "We wondered what had happened to you."

Fenella walked forward.

"Simon," she said, "we have a visitor. It's someone whom you used to know many years ago."

"So many years ago that it's almost uncomfortable to be reminded of it," Aunt Julie said.

She moved forward to where Simon stood a little way inside the door.

Simon turned his head sharply.

"Who's that?" he asked. "Who spoke then?"

There was a sudden edge to his voice.

"It's Miss McClelland," Fenella replied nervously. "Julie McClelland."

Simon seemed hardly to hear her. He turned his head in the direction from which Julie McClelland had last spoken.

"Speak," he said. "Say something again."

"Your daughter was introducing me," Aunt Julie said in a quiet voice.

Fenella knew she was nervous by the way the blood rose in her cheeks.

"As she said, it is many years since we met, but I daresay you remember me. I am Arline's sister, Julie."

"I remember your voice," Simon said, and his own shook.

Then out of the mists of the past Fenella remembered and knew that Julie's real resemblance to their Mother lay in the fact that their voices were identical.

● ● ●

"I like her," Moo said, sitting on the edge of the kitchen table and swinging her legs.

"Yes, she's nice," Fenella replied, rolling out the pastry for the pie she was making for lunch; "but I hope she isn't going to stay too long."

"Why?" Moo asked, and there was a touch of asperity in her voice.

"Well, for one thing, after to-day we are going to be servantless, and personally I find factory work far easier than running this house with so many people in it.

"Servantless!" Moo echoed. "What's happening to the old body we brought from Wetherby Court?"

"She's returning there to-night," Fenella replied; "she says the work is too hard for her and she's not used to it. When I think of how Nannie and I managed, it makes me laugh."

"Can't you get one of the others to take her place?" Moo suggested.

"I shouldn't think there's a chance. They are all used to doing things in a leisurely, comfortable manner. Besides, they're really Coleby servants, not mine, and they don't forget to let me know it."

"Heavens!" Moo exclaimed. "And I thought when you became a 'Lady' all our troubles were over."

"Then you thought wrong. As far as I can make out they are only just beginning."

"Oh, I don't think I should say that," Moo replied. "After all, Aunt Julie's going to be a kind of fairy godmother."

"Why, what has she said?" Fenella enquired.

"Well, she's asked me to go and stay with her as long as I like and whenever I like and she's promised to give me all sort of things I've always wanted.

"Clothes, of course, are impossible with coupons, but

165

she's going to have some of Mother's jewellery reset for you and me and our grandmother's furs remodelled. Oh, Fenella, it's exciting!"

Finella looked at the ecstatic expression on Moo's face and repressed a slight pang of jealousy as she realized that her younger sister's affection was now centred on someone else.

"Have you written to thank Raymond for sending her here?"

"I've written to tell him all about her," Moo said. "Wasn't it brave of him to go and visit the McClellands without having the slightest idea of what sort of reception he was going to have?

"Aunt Julie says that if our grandfather had been alive she's afraid that he would have turned Raymond out of the house."

"I think he sounds a horrid old man," Fenella said; "I've always thought so. Otherwise he wouldn't have had all these bitter, revengeful feelings against Simon all these years."

"Well, Simon seems to have forgotten them now. He obviously likes Aunt Julie. He's always asking for her when she isn't there and he sat listening for hours while she read to him last night."

"That's only because her voice is exactly the same as our Mother's."

"I wonder! Wouldn't it be marvellous, Fenella, if Simon settled down and married Aunt Julie."

"You've obviously been reading the women's magazines Nurse Bennett keeps buying," Fenella said scornfully. "Things don't happen like that in real life."

"But they might," Moo insisted. "After all, extraordinary, unusual things do happen to us, don't they? Look at Elaine, for instance."

"Yes, of course, there's Elaine," Fenella said soberly.

"Well, who knows what the future holds?" Moo said lightly.

Fenella put down the rolling-pin and looked at her younger sister.

"Moo," she asked earnestly, "you are happier, aren't you?"

"Happier?" Moo echoed. "I'm happy, frightfully happy, Fenella. I suppose I was rather awful the way I went on when it all happened—Elaine, I mean—but now you're married to Nicholas, who's the nicest man in all the world, and Aunt Julie's here, and there's such lots of things to look forward to, well I just couldn't be happier."

"I'm glad about that," Fenella said.

She couldn't prevent a light sigh escaping her.

"There's only one thing that worries me," Moo said, "and that is that you aren't really happy too. Oh, Fenella, do stop thinking about that stupid Rex."

"I don't think about him," Fenella said quickly.

"Oh yes, you do," Moo replied; "and I always know when you're doing it. You get a sort of far-away, wistful look in your eyes. It makes you look very pretty, but mournful, and somehow it's rather irritating—at least I should find it so if I was Nicholas."

"Well, you aren't Nicholas, so let's not worry about it," Fenella said tartly.

Moo got off the table and moving across to her sister suddenly put her arms round her neck.

"Oh, do like him, Fenella," she whispered, "do. He's so sweet, he is really."

"Really, Moo, don't be tiresome," Fenella said, pushing the child away. "You'd better let me finish this pastry or you'll have nothing to eat for lunch. It's time for elevenses. Go and see if Simon or Nurse want anything. I expect you've already asked Aunt Julie."

"I have," Moo answered, "and she doesn't. She's writing letters."

"Well, run away then and leave me alone. It really isn't the time of day to have a heart-to-heart talk about our souls, or our hearts for that matter."

"All right," Moo replied and wandered off, humming to herself.

'A few months ago,' Fenella thought, 'she'd have

been in tears because I snubbed her. She certainly has more confidence these days.'

She was glad of the change and yet it gave her a queer sense of loss. Moo had always clung to her, clung nervously and feverishly in a way which had made Fenella believe she was indispensable to her little sister.

Now Moo was learning to stand on her own feet, and although Fenella was glad about it she could not help feeling that it intensified her own loneliness.

She put the pastry on top of the fruit in the pie-dish and was just trimming in with a knife when she heard footsteps in the passage. She knew at once by the awkward, uneven sound of them who it was.

"Good morning, Nick," she said as her husband appeared in the doorway. "You're quite a stranger."

"I couldn't get over yesterday," Nick said. "I was at the aerodrome from first thing in the morning until midnight. I did try to telephone you about ten o'clock, but there was no asnwer.

"Someone said they thought they heard the telephone," Fenella said, "but we had the new wireless blaring. You gave it to Simon, so you've only yourself to blame. By the way, he's thrilled with it."

"I'm glad about that."

Fenella carried the pie across the kitchen and put it into the oven.

"You know it's strange," she said, "but I'd never have believed Simon could have behaved as he does."

"You mean being so calm about his blindness?" Nicholas asked.

"Calm is hardly the right word," Fenella said, shutting the oven door with a little bang. "I suppose really 'brave' is what I mean and yet it's more than that.

"It's the kind of super-sensitive courage which makes him determined that no one shall be sorry for him. He even makes a joke of his helplessness. Sometimes I don't know whether to laugh with him or cry for him."

"Your Father has never lacked courage."

"No, that's true; still, he's never worried before what anybody thought; he's always done exactly what he

168

wanted to do. Yet now I can see what he's thinking—
that his blindness is an embarrassment to other people
and he is determined to put them at their ease."

"I've got some news of another member of your family," Nicholas said hesitatingly.

"Of Raymond?" Fenella asked quickly, the idea that
her brother was in danger or injured coming immediately to her mind.

"No, good news and not about Raymond," Nicholas
replied. "Look at this."

He produced a *Daily Sketch* from his pocket. The
headlines read:
SURVIVORS FROM TORPEDOED SHIP LANDED
SAFELY IN A WEST OF ENGLAND PORT.

Nicholas pointed with his finger some way down the
paragraph and then read:

"Among the survivors of six days at sea in an open
lifeboat was Kay Prentis, the well-known Hollywood
film star and daughter of Simon Prentis, the famous artist."

"Kay!" Fenella exclaimed. "Then she's home! Oh,
where can we get hold of her?"

Nicholas turned over the paper to where the story
was contined on the back page.

"Here we are," he said. " 'Miss Kay Prentis, inter-
viewed last night at the Savoy Hotel, praised the hero-
ism of the seamen who had navigated the boat and
said . .'"

Fenella put down the paper.

"Kay's at the Savoy. Oh, let's ring her up. I'd no
idea she was coming home. How awful for her being
torpedoed!"

"Shall I put a call through for you?" Nicholas asked.

"Yes, please do," Fenella answered. "I'll tell Moo."

She picked up the paper and ran out of the room, not
waiting for the slower steps of her husband.

Simon as well as Moo was in a state of excitement
after Fenella had read the newspaper to them, and
when finally they got through to Kay at the Savoy Hotel

they all clustered round the telephone taking it in turns to speak to her.

"Why didn't you let us know you were coming home?" Fenella asked.

"It's a long story," Kay replied, "but I'll tell you all about it when I see you. Can I come down and stay?"

"But of course. When will you come—to-day?"

"I'll come to-morrow," Kay promised. "I've got to get some clothes first. I arrived in nothing but my night-gown, a pair of slacks and a fur coat. It was all I had time to put on before we left the ship."

"Oh, Kay, how awful! Were you frightened?"

"Absolutely terrified, except that it was all so unreal, like acting a bad part which seemed to go on and on interminably. But I'll tell you all about it, darlings. I'll be down to-morrow—meet me at the station."

"We will," Fenella promised.

She put down the receiver and turned to face the family.

"Do you realize we haven't seen Kay for eight years? We've got such a lot to tell her I can't think where we're going to begin."

Aunt Julie, who had joined the party grouped round the telephone, said tentatively:

"If your sister's coming I expect you would like me to go. I know how short of rooms you are."

Fenella, who had already thought that it might make it more convenient, was about to reply politely when Simon anticipated her.

"Of course you can't go," he said. "You must stay. Besides, it's only right you should meet the whole family."

"If you're quite certain I shan't be in the way," Aunt Julie said, obviously anxious to be pressed.

Moo rushed across to her and slipped an arm through hers.

"We couldn't bear you to go," she said with obvious sincerity. "Please don't leave us, Aunt Julie."

"Very well, then, I won't," Julie McClelland said.

170

Fenella fancied that there was relief as well as pleasure in her tone.

'Well, we'll manage somehow,' she thought to herself. 'Thank goodness, the nurseries are empty and the children at Wetherby Court.'

It was only when they all dispersed to different rooms, talking as they went, and she found herself alone with Nicholas, that she began to wonder about the domestic problem.

"I suppose you can't think of anyone who would like to come over and help me in the house?" she said to her husband.

"I'll find you someone," he promised. "I'm not going to have you do all this work."

Then he added: "I was beginning to hope that you'd come home."

"Home?" Fenella queried, forgetting for a moment that he was speaking of Wetherby Court. "Well, it doesn't look as though I'll be able to manage it, does it?"

"Have you spoken to your Father about coming to us?"

Fenella shook her head.

"I'm sorry, Nicholas, I haven't dared suggest it. You see, he loves being here because he knows his way about. It really is extraordinary how he can manage to get round the rooms and up the stairs all by himself. He'd never feel the same in your big house which is strange to him."

"Our house," Nicholas corrected. "I miss you, Fenella."

"Do you?" Fenella smiled at him.

For once she did not let herself shrink from his tone of intimacy.

"Particularly at the moment."

"Why?"

"The trials of the Cobra take place at the end of the week."

Fenella gave a little cry.

"Oh, Nick, how awful of me! I'd really forgotten all about it. I haven't asked you how it was getting along, have I, not for days."

"You've had a lot of things to occupy your mind," he said.

But Fenella was thoroughly ashamed of herself.

"You know how interested I am. Was that why you were kept at the aerodrome last night?"

Nicholas nodded.

"One or two things went wrong—nothing serious, but enough to be worrying. We've got Neville Earles, the famous test pilot, coming down. You've heard of him?"

"Of course," Fenella said. "Isn't it rather a compliment that he shoud test the Cobra?"

Nicholas's eyes shone.

"A tremendous compliment. It just shows what they think of it. We're pretty excited, Dick and I."

"Of course you are. Oh, Nick, shall I be able to see the test?"

"I was rather afraid you were going to ask me that," he said.

"It's impossible. I've tried to suggest that you might come and watch—not that there's much to see, the real test goes on up in the sky out of sight—but the Air Ministry regulations are pretty rigid."

"Well, I shall just have to stay at home and pray," Fenella said. "And I shall be praying for its success, you know that, Nick."

Nicholas looked at her.

"Do you really care a damn what happens to me one way or another?"

Fenella felt herself flush.

"Of course I do," she replied, making her eyes meet his unflinchingly.

Then suddenly she held out both her hands. "Don't make me rush my fences, Nick."

He took her hands, gripping them fiercely.

"I won't make you do anything as long as I've got a chance some time, some day. Have I got that, Fenella?"

Fenella's eyes fell before his, but she nodded her head an in a low whisper answered him.

"Yes, Nick."

"That's all I want to know. I'll be content with that."

He dropped her hands and she was free, but she did not want to move away from him. Instead she said hesitatingly:

"Are you doing anything to-day? Won't you stay here—we like having you."

She knew that she had pleased him.

"I've got to go up to the aerodrome this afternoon," he said, "but I'll come back for dinner if it won't be too much work for you, and that reminds me—I'll go and get you some help of some sort."

"I don't care what it's like as long as it's a pair of hands," Fenella said.

"You shall have them," Nicholas promised and went towards the front door.

Fenella followed him slowly; she watched him clamber laboriously into his car and waved as he drove off; then she stood for a moment with her hands in front of her eyes.

"Oh God! make me be decent to him," she prayed. "I must try—I must!"

If only she could be certain that Rex no longer had any power over her heart; but it was as if she must hold herself back from all feeling lest that which she had renounced should come sweeping back in a flood to hold her captive.

She thought of Rex going away from her and yet somehow the agony of losing him was no greater than the agony she was feeling at being unable to give Nicholas what he wanted.

She felt so helpless, so powerless to command and control herself and her own emotions.

Rex and Nicholas—two men, and she must fail them both.

● ● ●

Kay was quite unreal, Fenella thought.

She was exactly like someone who until then Fenella

had believed existed only in the imaginations of scenario writers and the more sensational novelists.

From the moment she stepped into the house everything and everybody seemed to revolve round her and be magnetized by her.

As the day passed, she was not certain secretly within herself whether or not she was really pleased to have Kay there. It was impossible for Fenella not to feel a little out of it or to enjoy being entirely supplanted by her elder sister.

From the moment Kay arrived she took command of everything.

The house seemed filled with her, everyone waiting to laugh at her jokes, to listen to her plans, to be—as Fenella put it to herself—nothing more or less than an applauding audience.

Nurse Bennett was in ecstasies about her, while Aunt Julie kept saying to Fenella over and over again:

"I never imagined there could be anyone like that out of a book. She's wonderful, dear, quite wonderful!"

Fenella knew that in complimenting her about Kay they thought they were making themselves pleasant, and when she was alone she had to admit that somewhere within her there was a streak of jealousy she had not hitherto suspected.

It was hard after all these years of running the house, of being the one person in the Prentis household to whom everyone turned either in sorrow, in happiness or in a difficulty, to find herself relegated very much to the background.

Kay shone. She was a star both on the screen and off it; she glittered and scintillated and everyone she met was apparently utterly content to let her queen it over them.

Nicholas came to dinner and so far as Fenella could see was as captivated as the rest of the household.

Certainly Kay set herself out to be particularly nice to Nicholas, and later in the evening when they were going up to bed she said to Fenella:

"My dear, don't ever complain to me about the dullness of the countryside when you can find anything so attractive as Nick living next door."

"Do you like him?" Fenella asked casually.

"I think he's adorable," Kay replied, "and if it wasn't for my Teddy I should lose my heart to him myself. Poor boy! what he must have gone through after that crash—but now he has you and that's something. Why isn't he staying here?"

It was typical of Kay, Fenella thought, to go straight to the point and to ask the one question she had been anticipating and dreading to hear.

"There isn't room," she said hastily. "You see how cramped we are."

"Oh yeah!" Kay said.

With an understanding look she kissed Fenella good night.

Alone in her own room Fenella undressed slowly, thinking over the events of the day and being a little shocked and not a little surprised at the resentment she found in her own heart.

'I am glad to see her—I am!' she told her reflection in the glass and knew that the words rang false.

The next day it was even harder for Fenella because Kay started planning and organizing the future for them all.

"It's like having a dynamo in the house," Simon said; but he meant it as a compliment while to Fenella it was very much the reverse.

Kay told them all what they were to do and it seemed to Fenella that they accepted her decisions as final.

"I'm going to take a flat in London as soon as I get back," Kay said. "It will have to be a large one because you, Simon, are coming up at once to stay with me. Now it's no use arguing—I want you to go to the very best oculist that it's possible to find.

"It's no use telling me your Service people are good, I've heard that story before. We'll start at the top of the profession and work down if needs be, but I'm not going to accept any verdict on your eyes as final until I've taken you to the real top-notchers.

"I've seen miracles happen before now and there's no reason why we shouldn't start trying to find a specialist who can work one. As for you, Moo, you've got to come to London because you're going to be my bridesmaid."

"Bridesmaid!" Moo said ecstatically.

"Yes, I'm going to have econe whether it's a Registry Office or not and we'll find you something attractive to wear whatever the Board of Trade has to say about it."

"Oh, Kay, how exciting!" Moo said.

"I thought you were going to stay with Aunt Julie?" Fenella couldn't resist saying it, pricking for a moment the bubble of excitement and elation which emulated from Kay.

"I am," Moo said, "but we must wait for Kay's wedding, mustn't we?"

"Of course," Kay interposed before Julie McClelland could speak, "and what's more, I'm expecting Aunt Julie to come too. You will, won't you?" she said, turning towards the older woman.

"I'd love to," the latter replied, "and if your flat isn't big enough, perhaps Moo could stay with me in an hotel?"

"Why don't you get a flat in London for yourself?" Kay asked.

"I never thought of it," Julie McClelland replied.

"Well, if you take my advice," Kay said, who had heard her story, "you'll shut up that castle of yours for the duration.

"Who wants to be buried alive in the North of Scotland anyway? You come to London and get some war work, and there's no reason why Moo shouldn't stay with you and go to a day school. She'd hate a boarding-school, and if she could do her lessons and come home at night that would make everyone happy, wouldn't it?"

Kay looked round with a self-satisfied expression.

'She doesn't really care,' Fenella thought to herself. 'It's just that she has so much energy that she has to push everyone along whether they want it or not.'

She waited for her own turn to come and sure enough Kay hadn't forgotten her.

"As for Fenella," she said, "she'll thank me for doing her a good turn. She'll be able to go back to her own lovely house with her charming husband.

"Poor Fenella! I think you people have treated her very badly all these years, letting her slog round being nothing more nor less than a drudge. I wish I'd known about it—I'd have been over here a long time ago altering things."

"I haven't been a drudge and I've liked it," Fenella said hotly.

She forgot all the times when she had grumbled, the long months when life had seemed lonely and unbearable.

"Nonsense!" Kay said briskly. "No one could like being an unpaid servant, because that's all you've been. Daddy, you ought to be ashamed of yourself. Fenella's lovely and ought to have had a chance to enjoy herself."

"You seem to forget," Simon answered, "that there has been a little thing called a war on over here and that with all your plans for London and gaiety you might remember that we may be raided. You haven't been through a blitz yet, my girl!"

"I expect I shall survive," Kay said cheerily, "and quite frankly, I'd rather be blitzed than bored."

"I seem to have heard that said before," Simon said cynically, "but it isn't true. I can promise you one thing—that you'll come running down to the country after the first bad raid on London."

"Well, I'll risk it," Moo said excitedly. "Oh, Kay, if you only knew how much I've wanted to go to London."

"Then the future's settled," Kay said. "You all agree, don't you?"

There was a chorus of assent. Only Fenella got up and slipped from the room while everyone else was talking.

She went out into the garden and stood by herself in

the shade of the walnut tree, looking down into the small water-lily pool which had been made long ago and was now overgrown through lack of attention.

It was there that Nicholas found her as he came limping across the lawn.

"I wondered where you'd got to," he said. "I saw you slip out of the room, but didn't know you'd gone for good."

"I was coming back in a few minutes," Fenella said.

She tried to speak naturally, but Nicholas was not deceived.

He put out his hand and touched her shoulder.

"What's the matter, Fenella?" he asked.

The garden was bathed in moonlight; it shone on the water-lily pond at their feet, transforming the ill-kept grass, the untrimmed bushes and weedy paths into a place of beauty and romance. Slowly Fenella turned to look at her husband.

"I'm a horrid person, Nick," she said, "because I'm resenting Kay arranging all these things for the family. I've looked after them up till now and yet I've never been able to give them one hundredth part of the happiness and the excitement they are going to find with Kay. It's mean of me, but I'm not pretending that I don't mind. I do."

She gave a little sob and turned away from him again, her mouth trembling. Nicholas's hand slipped from her shoulders down her arm and then she felt her fingers taken in a warm grasp.

"I understand," he said. "I, too, have often felt out of it in my life."

"It isn't exactly that," Fenella replied swiftly, somehow strangely content to leave her hand in his. "It isn't that I want anything for myself, it's just that I've liked being the person to give things. I've liked mothering the family, if one puts it that way."

Nicholas thought for a moment, then he said:

"Don't you think one's life always runs in cycles? Suddenly one gets to the end of one particular bit of it, but there's always something else to come on with which to start again."

Fenella stiffened. She knew what he was inferring—that her life now lay with him. In her bitterness she tried to hurt him.

"I wonder you don't say that I shall soon have another family to mother," she remarked caustically.

She released her hand from his, turning away with something of the petulance of a small child.

"I wouldn't be so presumptuous as to use the word 'soon'," Nicholas replied quietly.

Fenella's anger evaporated as quickly as it had risen.

"I'm sorry, Nick," she said. "That was horrid of me. You're trying to be nice, but I don't know what's the matter with me these days, I seem to be getting waspish and beastly. I'm out of step with everything and everybody."

"I know the remedy but I wouldn't dare suggest it," Nick said. "Come back to the house, they'll be wondering what's happened to you."

Fenella shrugged her shoulders.

"Let them," she said.

She felt somehow that she couldn't face Kay again.

'I'm jealous,' she told herself, 'jealous of her,' and she was ashamed.

Kay was so attractive; for Kay life was an easy, exciting adventure in which everything fell into its appointed place or else was just as easily forgotten.

'Things go smoothly for her,' Fenella thought, 'because she doesn't care enough. If she makes a mistake, whether it is in her work or her marriages, she cuts it out and starts again.

'Supposing,' she went on in her own mind, 'supposing I asked Nicholas for a divorce. Why not? We don't see eye to eye.'

Then the idea of losing him seemed startlingly bleak.

'If I hadn't got Nicholas, who would I have?' she wondered and impulsively turned towards him again.

"Don't take any notice of me to-night, Nick,' she

179

pleaded. "I've got what Nannie used to call 'an imp on my shoulder'."

He put out his hand towards her and then checked himself, as if he was half afraid she would resent the gesture.

"Shall I tell you what I think?" he asked.

"Yes, do."

"There are people in this world," he said, "who flow through other people's lives like a wide, steady river. There are others who come bursting in like a sudden shower of rain. One notices the rain; it's unexpected, it has an immediate effect on one, but the river is always there.

"You're like a river, Fenella; those who know you will always want and need you however much they may be taken up for the moment by the showers."

Nicholas had spoken with only a slight hesitancy, but Fenella knew that every word had been difficult for him to utter and yet it came straight from his heart.

She felt a sudden impulse of tenderness towards him.

"Thank you, Nick, that's sweet of you," she said, "and it's comforting—although I don't think Kay would like to be called a shower. She'd rather prefer to be a sunbeam or something very glittering like a flash-light."

"Aren't you being rather catty?" Nicholas asked, and Fenella nodded.

"Very, and I'm enjoying it."

They both laughed.

"We must go back," Fenella said and slipped her arm through her husband's. "Shall I tell you the nicest thing about you, Nick?"

"I'd like to hear it," he answered. "Nice things don't often come my way."

"Don't make me sorry for you," Fenella commanded. "It is that I can be honest with you and truthful, I don't have to pretend. I suppose there are very few people with whom one can be entirely natural, but I don't pretend to you, Nick—I let you see the worst of me."

"As long as I can also see the best," Nick murmured.

180

Then as they reached the side door into the house he stopped.

"Fenella, will you let me kiss you good night?"

Fenella felt herself shrink from him, then she forced a smile.

"Of course, Nick; why not?"

She lifted up her face slightly to his, the moon dazzled her eyes a little so that she closed them. But Nick did not kiss her. Instead he stood looking at her face, his arms by his side.

"You've been frank with me," he muttered after a moment. "Now I'll be frank with you. I want to kiss you—want to most damnably—but I'm not going to. Not until you want to. I've asked you now because I wanted to see what you'd say, but, Fenella—I'm not entirely a fool where you're concerned. Good night."

He turned away from her and, instead of entering the house, walked down the gravelled path which led to the front door. Fenella stood very still.

After a little time she heard his car start and drive away. She listened to the sound of it going down the drive, she caught a glimpse of its lights shining through the trees, and then it was gone. The garden lay before her bathed in moonlight, very empty and still.

Suddenly there was a burst of laughter coming through the open studio window. She gave a little sigh, turned and went into the house.

CHAPTER SEVEN

Fenella woke with a sense of foreboding. For a moment she lay in that no man's land between waking and sleeping, wondering why she felt oppressed and anxious—then she remembered.

It was the day that the Cobra was to be tested.

She got out of bed and dressed quickly. It was still early, the sun barely risen, the morning mists dispersing slowly in the garden. When she was ready she ran downstairs to the telephone.

She hardly expected Nick to be up, but it was his voice that answered her.

"I wanted to wish you the best of luck," she said.

"Thank you, Fenella."

His voice was slow and grave.

"Are you anxious?"

"I try not to be. Dick is supremely confident, but I'm afraid I feel rather like I felt when I went in to bat for Eton at Lords—very shaky about the knees."

"I didn't know you were a cricketer."

"I used to be."

'What an absurd conversation this is,' Fenella thought to herself.

Yet she knew that neither of them could find the right words to say to each other at this important moment.

"Well, I shall be thinking of you," she said. "Will you telephone me the moment you can?"

"I don't know when that will be," Nick replied. "Earles is arriving about noon; there will be various things for him to test and see first before he actually goes up. Anyway, I will telephone you the moment I know—you can be sure of that."

"Thank you. Good-bye, Nick."

"Good-bye."

He seemed to be waiting for something else. Fenella waited too, then hurriedly, rather self-consciously, she added:

"God bless you and the Cobra."

She put the receiver down before he could reply.

She walked slowly upstairs again to make her bed and tidy her room before she started to get breakfast for the rest of the household.

'This means so much to Nick,' she thought to herself. 'It must succeed—it must!'

She realized that her husband was suffering from a form of inferiority complex.

All his life he had been dominated by his mother and after such a brief period of independence in the Air Force he had come home ill and crippled to be swamped by Lady Coleby's vitality, to play the part he had played ever since childhood—second fiddle to her omnipotence.

The success of the Cobra, Fenella knew, would give him what he needed so much—the feeling of usefulness and of personal importance.

Within herself came the accusation that this need not have been so necessary had not Nick also a sense of inferiority where she was concerned. Had he not failed to win the love of his wife, to assert his rights, to gain his manhood in marriage?

'He knew what to expect when he married me,' she answered herself defiantly, yet felt that was no justification.

Nick's delicacy and sensitiveness where she was concerned had prevented him from behaving like a brute and forcing her pride into submission.

He had behaved, indeed, like a gentleman and had gained from it nothing but the bitterness of knowing his own weakness where she, Fenella, was concerned.

Fenella gave herself a mental shake. It was no use, she felt, reproaching herself at this moment, and yet the thought that she had treated Nick badly, in fact was treating him badly, persisted with her all through the morning.

She found herself wondering what would have been her attitude towards her husband had he been testing the aeroplane himself or, indeed, going up to fight against the enemy as he had fought in the past.

She wondered now whether she would have been shamed into spending the night with him before he departed.

Knowing Nick, she was sure he would not have slept last night.

She could imagine him moving about his room, hearing the chimes of the grandfather clock in the hall hour after hour, or trying to sleep, lying in the darkness with closed eyes, every muscle tense, every nerve in his body anticipating the flight of the Cobra, its silver wings moving against the blue sky of his imagination.

'I could at least have sat with him,' Fenella told herself.

She knew that her mind steered away dishonestly from a deeper implication.

All through the morning she thought of Nick. Twelve o'clock came and went, and slowly it seemed to her the minutes crept by until luncheon time.

It was easier when the whole household were gathered together to become absorbed in their chatter and talk and to forget if only momentarily the trial which might be taking place at that very moment.

After lunch Fenella and her Aunt sat talking but she could not keep her mind on the conversation. She kept thinking of Nicholas and the trials.

She looked at the clock over the mantelpiece; it was

after three o'clock. Surely he should have telephoned now? There must be something that he could have told her of what had taken place.

Supposing, just supposing things went wrong and Nicholas had no one to whom to turn, no one to help him through his darkest hour?

On an impulse Fenella said:

"I'm going over to Wetherby Court. Nick will go there to telephone me—I would like to be there when he arrives."

If Julie McClelland thought her sudden decision strange she was too wise to say so; instead she helped Fenella change her dress and promised to explain to the others where she had gone.

"I'll see about tea and dinner if you don't get back," she said, "so don't worry."

"I expect I shall be back," Fenella answered, but uncertainly.

For the first time in her life the comfort of her family had ceased to matter. They must manage, she thought.

She kissed her aunt and took up her handbag.

Fenella hurried down the stairs, she took her bicycle out of the shed by the back door and started off down the drive.

It took her twenty minutes to get to Wetherby Court and when she arrived there she half expected to see Nicholas waiting for her in the hall. She knew Aunt Julie would have told him that she was on her way if he had rung up in the meantime.

But there was no Nicholas, only Lady Coleby coming out of the drawing-room dressed in her Red Cross uniform as President of the County.

"What a surprise, Fenella," she exclaimed. "I had no idea you were coming over this afternoon."

"Nor had I," Fenella replied; "but I wanted to see Nicholas. Is he back yet?"

"No, he's still down at the aerodrome—at least, that's where he went this morning. I suppose you will wait for him? Tell Dawson to bring you some tea. I'm afraid I can't stop, I'm late as it is for a meeting in Melchester."

"Then I mustn't keep you," Fenella said.

She watched her mother-in-law go, pompous and slightly ridiculous in her uniform, a woman who must always cling, to the last gasp of her breath, to her power over her fellow creatures.

When she was alone Fenella did not ring for Dawson as she had been told, instead she wandered about the rooms downstairs. The house seemed empty and quiet.

She longed for the return of the children whom she knew would have gone out for a walk with Nannie, and then suddenly she felt she could bear it no longer.

She must know what had happened. She must find something to ease the weight of anxiety within her breast.

She had a premonition of something being wrong, and while she told herself it was only imagination the feeling persisted.

She started to walk down the drive which led towards the aerodrome. Every moment she expected to see Nicholas's car approaching, but there was no sign of him.

She turned out of the drive into the country lane and a few minutes later reached the aerodrome. Opposite the gates there was a small parking place.

Fenella looked and saw among the half a dozen cars parked there Nicholas's small green two-seater.

She went towards it, debating within herself what she should do, and then at that moment her heart gave a sudden leap, for she heard coming down the lane the clanging of an ambulance.

She stood very still, hearing the car come nearer and watching it, as if in a dream, turn in at the gates of the aerodrome.

Her premonition, then, had not been wrong; something had happened, something she had feared with an inexplicable sixth sense.

She waited. How long she waited afterwards she had no idea. Eventually she sat down on the running board of the car.

It must have been two hours later that Nick came out through the gates of the aerodrome. People had come and gone in the meantime, cars had approached and driven off, but Fenella had not heeded them.

She had been waiting for one person and for one person only.

And then she saw him. A glance at his face told her what she already knew. He limped across to the car, taking his key out of his pocket as he came.

Fenella got slowly to her feet; she was vaguely conscious as she did so of being cramped and stiff.

It seemed to her at that moment that she had waited an eternity for Nick, an eternity in which so much had happened within her that the whole world so far as she was concerned was completely changed.

She said nothing. Nick looked at her but did not speak, and she knew that he was neither glad nor surprised to see her; he was past any feeling save that of numbness and despair.

He opened the door and leaning across unbolted the one which opened on her side. She got in and without saying a word they drove off.

They drove side by side in silence until at last they came to the bend in the tree-shaded drive and Wetherby Court lay before them, grey and lovely in the sunshine, the lake shimmering like a bowl of silver at its feet.

Then Nicholas drew the car up on the grass and switched off the engine.

"Do you want to know what happened?" he asked in a harsh voice.

A voice so raw with feeling that it hurt Fenella almost physically to hear it.

For one wild moment she was afraid—afraid to speak, afraid to answer him, and then at last she knew the right way, the way to help, the way to assuage this new wound.

"No, don't tell me," she said, "don't speak about it. I know—know what's happened. Oh, Nicholas, I'm so sorry!"

She reached out her arms as she spoke and drew his head down towards her.

She was not conscious of what she said, only of her

action in drawing him to her, of giving deliberately something of herself to him in the very gesture.

For a moment Nicholas seemed to resist her until suddenly, as if the hard armour of his pride collapsed, he turned towards her, his head dropping lower until his eyes were hidden against her neck, and she heard his voice, low and broken:

"It's failed, Fenella—it's failed."

"I know, I know," Fenella heard herself saying, "but it doesn't matter. You can start work again, everything can't be wrong; there must be just one small thing you hadn't allowed for, hadn't anticipated."

Slowly she felt his arms tighten round her.

"That's what Dick said," he answered, "but, Fenella—I believed in the Cobra. It meant so much. I felt it was my plane—yours and mine."

She felt him draw a deep breath at the words.

"Perhaps I haven't had enough part in it," she said.

Then the words died on her lips as she felt something warm and wet against her neck and knew Nick was crying.

Nick crying! An instinct which had made her always want to mother those around her swelled up within her at that moment to envelop and encircle this young husband of hers for all time.

She tightened her arms about him pressing her cheek against his.

"Don't, darling . . . don't!" she begged in a voice she would have used to a child. "We'll start again . . . we'll do it together, you and I. Just you and I, Nick . . . if you'll let me."

He moved, straightening himself, and now he was looking down at her, the tears unashamedly in his eyes and on his cheeks.

She glanced up at him and was held spellbound by the look in his eyes, by the sudden hope, radiant and shining, which was there in his expression.

'So that's what love looks like,' she thought involuntary, and then felt her own heart singing.

She could make Nick look like this, she could keep him from despair and despondency, could turn his agony into joy. She saw his lips move.

"Say that again," he said, "please say that again."

He spoke almost in a whisper, but Fenella's answer rang out clear and courageous:

"We'll do it together, darling—you and I."

● ● ●

It was very quiet in the big bedroom in Wetherby Court and Fenella could hear her heart beating.

She was waiting, waiting breathless for the door to open.

It seemed to her that this was a moment she had been moving towards all her life. It had been a slow movement but relentless and inevitable.

Nicholas had said she was like a river—wide and steady. She had been neither in the past but now that was what she wanted to be, so that she could help Nicholas!

She felt as if all the emotions—protective, inspiring, sustaining and comforting she had felt for Moo and the children, for Simon and Raymond had all crystalized themselves in one—into which she felt for Nicholas!

She wanted to give him so much more than she had even given before, so much more than she had ever been capable of giving.

Then in a sudden fear she wondered if it was too late?

Had she hurt him so much and so often he no longer trusted her?

She was only frightening herself. She remembered the hope in his eyes despite the tears and the wonder in his voice.

He still loved her—he must love her.

But still the fear was there. Did he realize she was waiting for him?

She heard the door open and saw Nicholas coming across the room to her.

She could not see the expression on his face because she had left only one candle alight.

Nicholas reached her and sat down on the side of the bed.

"Fenella," he said tentatively.

She knew he was afraid that after all she didn't want him. Afraid of being hurt yet again.

Fenella put out her hand towards his and felt his fingers grip it almost painfully.

"I have . . . something to . . . tell . . . you," she said and her voice was very low.

"I'm listening," Nicholas replied.

Fenella drew in a deep breath.

"But . . . you are . . . so far away . . . it is very . . . secret."

She felt him stiffen.

Then slowly as if he expected her to stop him, he got into bed and took her in his arms.

Suddenly she was pressing herself against him clinging to him.

"Oh Nicholas . . . Nicholas," she whispered, "I've been so stupid . . . so horrid . . . but I didn't understand until . . . to-day . . . how much you mean to me . . . how much I need you . . ."

Her voice broke on a sob.

"Love me . . . please . . . please love me . . . and help me . . . I want to belong . . . to you . . . to work with you . . . to share . . ."

The tears were running down her cheeks.

"My darling, my sweet, my own adorable little wife," Nicholas said in a voice she had never heard before. "I love you—I worship you."

He was kissing her eyes, the tears on her cheeks, the softness of her neck before he paused. Fenella knew why.

She turned her face up to his.

"I love you . . Nicholas . . I love you."

Then his lips were on hers and she knew a rapture and ecstasy she had never known before.

'This time it's love . . . real love,' she thought.

Then a sudden flame flickered into life to meet the fire burning in Nicholas.

It was so perfect, so utterly divine, she could only draw him closer and still closer . .

They were no longer two people but one.

This was love!

are you missing out on some great Pyramid books?

You can have any title in print at Pyramid delivered right to your door! To receive your Pyramid Paperback Catalog, fill in the label below (use a ball point pen please) and mail to Pyramid . . .